Rand McNally and Company

Indexed map of Indiana

showing the railroads in the state, and the express company doing

business over each, also, counties, islands, lakes and rivers, together with

every post office, railroad station or town, carefully indexed

Rand McNally and Company

Indexed map of Indiana
showing the railroads in the state, and the express company doing business over each, also, counties, islands, lakes and rivers, together with every post office, railroad station or town, carefully indexed

ISBN/EAN: 9783337368661

Printed in Europe, USA, Canada, Australia, Japan

Cover: Foto ©Andreas Hilbeck / pixelio.de

More available books at **www.hansebooks.com**

Rand, McNally & Co.'s

INDEXED MAP

OF

INDIANA

SHOWING THE

RAILROADS IN THE STATE,

And the Express Company doing business over each,

ALSO,

Counties, Townships,

LAKES AND RIVERS,

TOGETHER WITH EVERY

Post Office, Railroad Station or Town,
carefully indexed, referring to the
exact location where each may
be found on the Map.

CHICAGO:

Rand, McNally & Co., Printers and Engravers,

77 and 79 Madison Street.

Explanation of Abbreviations.

—Miles. N—North. S—South. E—East. W—West.

* No Town.

The figures before names of towns denote population, either census of 1870, or estimated.

The townships are numbered on the Map. The corresponding numbers designating the names, are found in the first column of figures before list of township names under each County.

The letters and figures following names, refer to that point on the map at which lines drawn from marginal figures top and bottom, and letters upon either side of map, would cross each other at right angles.

For example, to find "*New York City D 5,*" let the diagram below represent the map. New York is seen near the crossing of lines D—D and 5—5.

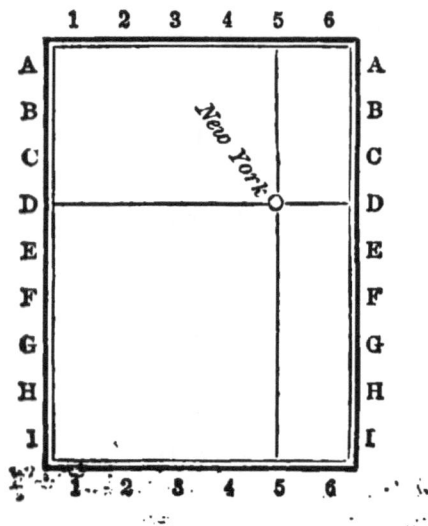

INDIANA RAILROADS.

Anderson, Lebanon & St. Louis.
Anderson (O 13) to Lebanon (K 13), and in course of construction to Waveland (G 14).

Baltimore & Ohio. American Express.
Chicago (D 3) to Chicago Junction, Ohio, leaving the State near St. Joe (T 6).
☞ See Rand, McNally & Co.'s Maryland.

Cairo & Vincennes. Adams Express.
Vincennes (D 21) to Cairo, Ill., leaving the State near St. Francisville, Ill. (D 22).
☞ See Rand, McNally & Co.'s Illinois.

Chicago, Danville & Vincennes.
(See Chicago & Eastern Illinois.)
☞ See Rand, McNally & Co.'s Illinois.

Chicago & Eastern Illinois. American Express.
Coal Creek (E 13) to Bismarck Junction, Ill. (D 12).
☞ See Rand, McNally & Co.'s Illinois.

Chicago & Lake Huron. American Express.
Valparaiso (G 5) to Lansing, Mich., leaving the State near Granger (M 3).
☞ See Rand, McNally & Co.'s Michigan.

Cincinnati, Hamilton & Dayton.
United States Express.
Indianapolis (M 15) to Cincinnati, Ohio, (V 19), leaving the State at College Corner (U 16).
☞ See Rand, McNally & Co.'s Ohio.

Cincinnati, Lafayette & Chicago.
American Express.
Lafayette (H 11) to Kankakee, Ill (B 7).

Cincinnati, Richmond & Ft. Wayne.
Operated by the Grand Rapids & Indiana.
Richmond (T 14) to Ft Wayne (S 7).

Cincinnati, Rockport & Southwestern.
Adams Express.
Rockport (G 26) to Jasper (H 23).

Cincinnati & Terre Haute.
Terre Haute (E 17) to Clay City (G 18), and in course of construction to Worthington (H 19).

Cincinnati, Wabash & Michigan.
United States Express.
Goshen (O 4) to Anderson (O 13).

RAILROADS—continued

Cleveland, Columbus, Cincinnati & Indianapolis.   United States Express.

Indianapolis (M 15) to Gallon, Ohio, leaving the State at Union City (U 12).
☞ See Rand, McNally & Co.'s Ohio.

Detroit, Eel River & Illinois.   American Express.

Logansport (K 9) to Butler (T 5).

Evansville & Crawfordsville.   Adams Express.

Evansville (D 25) to Terre Haute (E 17).

Evansville, Terre Haute & Chicago.

E., T. H. & C. Express.
Terre Haute (E 17) to Danville, Ill. (D 13), leaving the State near Gessie (E 13).

Fairland, Franklin & Martinsville.

American Express.
Fairland (N 16) to Martinsville (K 17).

Frankfort & Kokomo.   American Express.

Kokomo (M 10) to Frankfort (J 12).

Ft. Wayne, Jackson & Saginaw.

American Express.
Ft. Wayne (S 7) to Jackson, Mich , leaving the State at State Line Station (T 3).
☞ See Rand, McNally & Co.'s Michigan.

Ft. Wayne, Muncie & Cincinnati.

American Express
Ft. Wayne (S 7) to Connersville (S 16).

Grand Rapids & Indiana.   United States Express.

Ft. Wayne (S 7) to Petoskey, Mich., leaving the State near Lima (Q 3).

CINCINNATI, RICHMOND & FT. WAYNE R. R.
Richmond (T 14) to Ft. Wayne (S 7).
☞ See Rand, McNally & Co.'s Michigan.

Indiana & Illinois Central.

Changed to Indianapolis, Decatur & Springfield.

Indiana North & South.   United States Express.

Attica (F 12) to Veedersburgh (F 13).

Indianapolis, Bloomington & Western.

United States Express.
Indianapolis (M 15) to Peoria, Ill., leaving the State near Mound City (E 13).
☞ See Rand, McNally & Co.'s Illinois.

RAILROADS—continued.

Indianapolis, Cincinnati & La Fayette.
American Express.
La Fayette (H 11) to Cincinnati, Ohio, (V 19).

Indianapolis, Decatur & Springfield.
American Express.
Coloma (F 15) to Decatur, Ill., leaving the State near Dana (E 15), and in course of construction to Rockville (F 15).
☞ See Rand, McNally & Co.'s Illinois.

Indianapolis, Peru & Chicago.
United States Express.
Michigan City (H 3) to Indianapolis (M 15).

Indianapolis & St. Louis. American Express.
Indianapolis (M 15) to St Louis, Mo, leaving the State near Sanford (D 16).

Indianapolis & Sullivan.
In course of construction from Sullivan (E 19) to Indianapolis (M 15).

Indianapolis & Vincennes.
Operated by the Pittsburgh, Cincinnati & St. Louis Railway.
Vincennes (D 21) to Indianapolis (M 15).

Jeffersonville, Madison & Indianapolis.
American Express.
Indianapolis (M 15) to Louisville, Ky (O 24).
Columbus (N 18) to Madison (Q 21)
Columbus (N 13) to Cambridge City (S 15).
Jeffersonville (O 24) to New Albany (N 24).

La Fayette, Muncie & Bloomington.
United States Express.
Muncie (Q 12) to Bloomington, Ill., via La Fayette (H 11).

Lake Erie, Evansville & Southwestern.
Adams Express.
Evansville (D 25) to Boonville (F 25), and in course of construction to Huntingburgh (H 23).

Lake Shore & Michigan Southern.
United States Express.
Chicago (D 3) to Buffalo, N. Y., leaving the State near Butler (T 5)
Elkhart (N 8) to White Pigeon, Mich. (P 8).
☞ See Rand, McNally & Co.'s Ohio.

Logansport, Crawfordsville & Southwestern.
American Express.
Logansport (K 9) to Terre Haute (E 17).

Louisville, New Albany & Chicago.
Michigan City (H 3) to Green Castle (H 16)..American Express.
Green Castle (H 16) to New Albany (N 24).......Adams Express.

RAILROADS—continued.

Louisville, New Albany & St. Louis Air Line.

Adams Express·

Princeton (D 23) to Albion, Ill., leaving the State at Mount Carmel, Ill. (C 23), and in course of construction to New Albany (N 24).

Michigan Central.   American Express.

Chicago (D 3) to Detroit, Mich., leaving the State near Corymbo (I 3).
Lake (F 4) to Joliet, Ill. (A 4).
South Bend (L 4) to Niles, Mich. (L 3).
☞ See Rand, McNally & Co 's Michigan.

Ohio & Mississippi.   Adams Express.

Cincinnati, Ohio, (U 19) to St. Louis, Mo , leaving the State at Vincennes (D 21).
North Vernon (P 19) to Louisville, Ky. (O 24).
☞See Rand, McNally & Co.'s Illinois.

Pittsburgh, Cincinnati & St. Louis.

Chicago (D 3) to Richmond (T 14). ....American Express.
State Line (D 9) to Union City (U 12)..... United States Express.
Indianapolis (M 15) to Richmond (T 14) ..United States Express.

INDIANAPOLIS & VINCENNES R. R.
Vincennes (D 21) to Indianapolis (M 15)........Adams Express.
☞See Rand, McNally & Co.'s Ohio.

Pittsburgh, Ft. Wayne & Chicago.

Adams Express.

Chicago (D 3) to Van Wert, Ohio, (V 8), leaving the State near Monroeville (T 8).
☞ See Rand, McNally & Co.'s Ohio.

St. Louis, Bloomfield & Louisville.

Bedford (K 20) to Linton (F 19), and in course of construction to Sullivan (E 19).

St. Louis & Southeastern.   Adams Express.

Evansville (D 25) to St Louis, Mo , leaving the State near Upton (B 25).
☞ See Rand, McNally & Co 's Illinois.

St. Louis, Vandalia, Terre Haute & Indian-apolis.   American and Adams Expresses.

Indianapolis (M 15) to St Louis, Mo., leaving the State near Farrington (D 17).

Wabash.   United States Express.

Toledo, Ohio, to Hannibal, Mo., entering the State near Woodburn (T 7), leaving at State Line (D 12).
☞ See Rand, McNally & Co.'s Illinois.

COUNTIES
and Townships.

ADAMS COUNTY.
Pop. 13327 ....T 9

1.	865.	Union..........T	8
2.	1252.	Root ....T	8
3.	996.	Preble.........S	8
4.	508.	Kirkland.......S	9
5.	3691.	Washington ..T	9
6.	1025.	St. Mary's ....T	9
7.	620.	Blue Creek ....T	9
8.	960.	Monroe ....T	9
9.	824.	French.........S	9
10.	935.	Hartford ....S	10
11.	957.	Wabash........T	10
12.	494.	Jefferson ..... T	10

ALLEN COUNTY.
Pop. 51070 ....S 7

1.	420.	Scipio.... .....U	6
2.	1749.	Springfield.....T	6
3.	1713.	Cedar Creek ...S	6
4.	1230.	Perry..........S	6
5.	24510.	Eel River ......R	6
6.	1809.	Lake ....R	7
7.	1628.	Washington ...R	7
8.	1373.	St. Joseph.....S	7
9.	1183.	Milan ....T	7
10.	894.	Maumee ....T	7
11.	202.	Jackson ....T	7
12.	1415.	Jefferson ......T	7
13.	3300.	Adams ....S	7
14.	1742.	Wayne ....R	7
15.	906.	Aboit ....R	7
16.	1471.	La Fayette ....R	8
17.	1280.	Pleasant ....S	8
18.	1319.	Marion ....S	8
19.	1278.	Madison ....T	8
20.	2568.	Monroe ....T	8

BARTHOLOMEW COUNTY.
Pop. 27761 ....N 18

1.	4056.	Haw Creek ....O	18
2.	1513.	Flat Rock .....N	18
3.	1652.	German........N	18
4.	767	Nineveh.... ..M	18
5.	1008.	Union ....M	18
6.	1282.	Harrison ......M	18
7.	8991.	Columbus .....N	18
8.	775.	Clay...........O	18
9.	1133.	Clifty ....O	18
10.	1203.	Rock Creek....O	18
11.	1684.	Sand Creek....N	19
12.	2247.	Wayne ....N	19
13.	747.	Ohio ....M	19
14.	673.	Jackson.......M	19

BENTON COUNTY.
Pop. 6434 ....F 10

1.	452.	Gilboa ....G	9
2.	810.	Union........F	9
3.	546.	Richland ......E	9

Pop. Counties—continued.

4.	433.	York ....E	9
5.	193.	Parish Grove ..E	10
6.	278.	Prairie ....F	10
7.	523.	Pine...........G	10
8.	776.	Bolivar ....G	10
9.	2058.	Oak Grove ....F	10
10.	835.	Grant ....E	10
11.		Hickory Grove.E	10

BLACKFORD COUNTY.
Pop. 7624 ....R 11

1.	1680.	Harrison.......R	10
2.	1008.	Washington ...Q	10
3.	3157.	Licking ....Q	11
4.	1479.	Jackson ....R	11

BOONE COUNTY.
Pop. 23324 ....K 13

1.	1786.	Marion L	13
2.	1220.	Clinton ....K	13
3.	1391.	Washington ...J	13
4.	4664.	Sugar Creek ...J	13
5.	1675.	Jefferson......J	13
6.	6471.	Centre.........K	13
7.	1343.	Worth..........K	13
8.	1057.	Union..........L	13
9.	3283.	Eagle L	14
10.	1109.	Perry ....K	14
11.	1209.	Harrison ......J	14
12.	3116.	Jackson.......J	14

BROWN COUNTY.
Pop. 9116 ....L 18

1.	2011	Hamblin.......M	18
2.	1750	Jackson........L	18
3.	2622	Washington ...L	18
4.	2018.	Van Buren ....M	19
5.	683.	Johnson........L	19

CARROLL COUNTY.
Pop. 20576 ....J 10

1.	920.	Washington...K	10
2.	1605.	Rock Creek ...J	10
3.	1325.	Adams ....J	9
4.	917.	Jefferson.......I	9
5.	1429.	Tippecanoe I	10
6.	6621.	Deer Creek ....J	10
7.	1777.	Jackson........J	10
8.	1046	Carrollton.....K	10
9.	910.	Monroe ....J	10
10.	727.	Madison ....J	10
11.	949.	Clay ....J	11
12.	1122.	Democrat......J	11
13.	1198	Burlington ....K	11

CASS COUNTY.
Pop. 28130............K 9

1.	807	Adams L	8
2.	993.	Bethlehem L	8
3.	1171.	Harrison ......K	8
4.	1568.	Boone..........K	8
5.	13476.	Jefferson ......J	9

Pop. Counties—continued.

6.	904.	Noble	K	9
7	160	Eel	L	9
8.	814	Clay	L	9
9.	1003.	Miami	L	9
10.	1808.	Tipton	L	9
11.	1220.	Washington	L	9
12	1021	Clinton	K	9
13.	1271.	Deer Creek	L	10
14	1909.	Jackson	L	10

CLARKE COUNTY.

Pop. 27979 .... O 22

1.	763	Bethlehem	Q	22
2	1357.	Washington	P	22
3.	1860.	Oregon	P	22
4	1863	Monroe	O	22
5.	720	Wood	N	23
6.	692.	Carr	O	23
7	1022.	Union	O	22
8.	5498	Charlestown	O	23
9	679	Owen	P	22
10.	1116	Silver Creek	O	23
11.	1598.	Utica	O	23
12	11301.	Jeffersonville	O	23

CLAY COUNTY.

Pop. 25141 .... G 17

1	5190	Van Buren	G	16
2.	5517.	Brazil	G	16
3.	868	Dick Johnson	F	16
4	3379.	Posey	F	17
5.	1711.	Jackson	G	17
6.	596.	Cass	H	17
7.	2473.	Washington	H	17
8	1605.	Sugar Ridge	G	17
9.	1340.	Perry	F	17
10.	2241.	Harrison	G	18
11.	1220.	Lewis	F	18

CLINTON COUNTY.

Pop. 21645 .... J 12

1.	1692.	Warren	K	11
2.	1118	Owen	J	11
3.	2257.	Ross	J	11
4.	865	Madison	J	11
5.	1387.	Washington	J	12
6.		Center	J	12
7.	2047.	Michigan	K	12
8.	1666.	Johnson	L	12
9.	961	Sugar Creek	L	12
10.	1407	Kirklin	K	12
11.	6407.	Jackson	J	12
12.	1835	Perry	J	12

CRAWFORD COUNTY.

Pop. 11009 .... J 23

1.	1214.	Whiskey Run	L	23
2.	757	Liberty	K	23
3	1327.	Sterling	K	23
4.	1253	Patoka	J	23
5.	652.	Johnson	J	23

Pop. Counties—continued.

6.	1082.	Union	J	24
7.	2813.	Jennings	K	24
8.	1150.	Ohio	K	25
9.	761.	Boone	K	25

DAVIESS COUNTY.

Pop. 21813 .... G 21

1.	1600.	Madison	H	20
2	865.	Elmore	G	20
3	733.	Steele	F	21
4.	1170.	Bogard	G	21
5	1225	Van Buren	H	21
6	3127.	Barr	G	21
7	9312.	Washington	F	21
8.	893.	Veale	F	22
9	1094	Harrison	G	22
10.	1799.	Reeve	H	22

DEARBORN COUNTY.

Pop. 32355 .... T 19

1.	1066.	Harrison	T	18
2.	832.	Logan	T	18
3	1903.	Kelso	T	18
4	1368.	Jackson	S	18
5	986	York	T	18
6.	1120	Miller	T	18
7.	6589.	Lawrenceb'gh	T	19
8.	2029	Manchester	T	19
9.	2596	Sparta	S	19
10.	1250.	Hogan	T	19
11.	10258.	Centre	T	19
12.	510.	Washington	T	19
13	1269.	Clay	S	19
14.	556	Cesar Creek	S	20

DECATUR COUNTY.

Pop. 23266 .... P 18

1.	1630	Fugit	Q	17
2.	828.	Clinton	Q	17
3.	2331.	Adams	P	17
4.	2596.	Clay	P	16
5	8104.	Washington	Q	17
6.	1687.	Salt Creek	Q	18
7.	2315	Marion	Q	18
8.	2029.	Sand Creek	P	18
9.	1746.	Jackson	P	18

DE KALB COUNTY.

Pop. 20807 .... T 5

1.	603.	Troy	U	5
2.	1243.	Franklin	T	5
3.	1342.	Smithfield	S	5
4.	1554.	Fairfield	S	5
5	2243.	Richland	S	5
6	6281.	Union	S	5
7.	2296.	Wilmington	T	5
8.	584.	Stafford	U	5
9.	812.	Newville	U	5
10.	1472.	Concord	T	6
11.	1141.	Jackson	S	6
12.	1209.	Butler	S	6

Counties—continued.

DELAWARE COUNTY.
Pop. 23543...........Q 12

1.	1140.	Niles...........R	11
2.	1244.	Union..........Q	11
8.	1190.	Washington ..P	11
4.	1400.	Harrison ......P	12
5.	1129.	Hamilton ....Q	12
6.	1210.	Delaware......R	12
7	1637.	Liberty........R	12
8	8890.	Centre ....Q	12
9.	1880.	Mt. Pleasant...P	12
10.	1413	Salem ....P	13
11.	1247.	Monroe ....Q	13
12.	1163.	Perry .... R	13

DUBOIS COUNTY.
Pop. 14223............H 23

1	1622	Columbia.......I	22
2.	1590.	Harbison......H	22
8.		Boone..........G	22
4		Madison ...... G	23
5.	4147	Bainbridge.....H	23
6.		Marion........ H	23
7.	2046.	Hall............ I	23
8.		Jefferson I	23
9.		Jackson........H	23
10.	3086.	Patoka..........H	23
11.		Cass............G	24
12.	1732.	Ferdinand.....H	24

ELKHART COUNTY.
Pop. 36332............N 4

1.	906.	York...........O	3
2.	2072.	Washington.. N	3
8	922.	Osolo..........N	3
4.	549.	Cleveland.....M	3
5.	749.	Baugo.........M	4
6.	12324.	Concord.......N	4
7.	982.	Jefferson ......O	4
8.	1709.	Middlebury ...O	4
9	2739.	Clinton ....N	4
10.	5236.	Elkhart........N	4
11.	1655.	Harrison......N	4
12.	1394.	Olive ....M	4
13.	1049.	Locke..........M	5
14.	1221	Union ......N	5
15.	1434.	Jackson ......O	5
16.	1391.	Benton........O	5

FAYETTE COUNTY.
Pop. 10991............R 16

1.	947.	Posey ....R	15
2.	601.	Fairview ......R	15
3.	867.	Harrison ......R	15
4.	671	Waterloo ......S	15
5.	836.	Jennings...... S	16
6.	4073.	Connersville . R	16
7.	681.	Orange ....R	16
8.	929.	Columbia......R	16
9.	1186	Jackson....... S	16

FLOYD COUNTY.
Pop. 23300............N 23

Pop. Counties—continued.

1.	17698.	New Albany...N	24
2.	1576	La Fayette ....N	23
8.	1814.	Greenville....N	23
4.	1424.	Georgetown...N	23
5.	793.	Franklin......N	24

FOUNTAIN COUNTY.
Pop. 20801............F 13

1	663.	Davis ....G	12
2	4881	Logan..........F	12
8	1759	Richland.......G	12
4	867.	Shawnee........F	12
5	5295.	Troy...........E	13
6.	1284.	Wabash........E	13
7.	522.	Van Buren.... F	13
8.	1802.	Cain............G	13
9.	1321.	Jackson........G	13
10.	1491.	Mill Creek... .F	13
11.	916.	Fulton........ E	13

FRANKLIN COUNTY.
Pop. 24575............S 17

1.	675	Bath...........T	16
2.	845	Fairfield ......T	16
3.	801.	BloomingGroveS	16
4.	3159.	Laurel.........S	16
5	974.	Posey.........R	17
6.	1223.	Salt Creek.... R	17
7.	1222.	Metamora......S	17
8.	6385	Brookville....S	17
9.	1513	Springfield.....T	17
10.	1467.	Whitewater ...T	17
11.	1796.	Highland......T	17
12.	1488.	Butler ....S	17
13.	3327.	Ray............R	17

FULTON COUNTY.
Pop. 14841............L 7

1.	1252.	New Castle....M	7
2	1314	Richland L	7
8.	745.	AubbeenaubbeeK	7
4.	1200.	Union ....K	7
5.	5841.	Rochester L	7
6.	1919.	Henry .... M	7
7.	1429.	Liberty L	8
8.	1131	Wayne ...... K	8

GIBSON COUNTY.
Pop. 22291............D 23

1.	757.	Washington.. E	23
2.	3374	White River.. D	23
3.	442	Wabash ....B	24
4.	3643.	Montgomery . C	24
5.	7595.	Patoka........D	24
6		Centre ....E	23
7	2233.	Columbia......E	23
8.	1626.	Barton........E	24
9.	2616	Johnson.......D	24

GRANT COUNTY.
Pop. 21600............P 10

| 1. | 1110. | Van Buren ....P | 10 |

Pop. Counties—continued.

2	1139	Washington....P	10
3.	1575	Pleasant.......O	10
4.	1065.	Richland......N	10
5	841.	Sims ....N	10
6.	1471	Franklin.......O	10
7.	4299	Centre.........P	10
8	1047.	Monroe ....P	10
9	2258	Mill ....P	11
10	1398	Jefferson...... Q	11
11.	2323.	Fairmount... P	11
12.	1989	Liberty........O	11
13.	1115.	Green.........N	11

GREENE COUNTY.
Pop. 20170 ....H   19

1.	2059.	Beech Creek.. I	19
2.	1321.	Highland .....H	19
3.	501	Eel River.....H	19
4.	1318.	Jefferson ..... G	19
5	670.	Smith .... G	19
6.	1104.	Wright ....F	19
7	1240.	Stockton...... F	19
8	532.	Grant .... G	19
9	780	Fairplay.......G	19
10	2799.	Richland ..... H	19
11	1870	Centre.........I	19
12	1969.	Jackson I	20
13.	1677.	Taylor........ H	20
14	819.	Cass...........H	20
15.	640.	Washington ..G	20
16.	841	Stafford ....F	20

HAMILTON COUNTY.
Pop. 24424 ... .M   13

1	2047.	White River . N	12
2.	4474	Jackson.......M	13
3.	2178	Adams.,.......L	13
4.	4198	Washington. ..L	13
5.	5752.	Noblesville....M	13
6.	1398.	Wayne.........N	13
7.	1533.	Fall Creek....N	14
8.	1134.	Delaware......M	14
9	1413.	Clay.. L	14

HANCOCK COUNTY.
Pop. 18421...........O   15

1.	1329.	Brown ....P	14
2.	1177.	Green........O	14
3.	2809	Vernon ......N	14
4	1227.	Buck Creek...N	15
5.	5376	Center ....O	15
6.	2420.	Jackson......P	14
7	1125.	Blue River...O	15
8.	1061.	Brandywine....O	15
9.	1897.	Sugar Creek ..N	15

HARRISON COUNTY.
Pop. 21890...........M | 24

1.	1426.	Morgan..... M	23
2	1193	Blue River .. L	23
3	1310.	Spencer L	24
4.	1400.	Jackson.......M	23

Pop. Counties—continued.

5.	1765.	Franklin......M	24
6.	2371.	Posey.........N	25
7.	1025.	Webster... ..M	25
8.	4479.	Harrison......M	24
9.	996.	Scott..........L	24
10.	1176.	Washington ...L	25
11.	1615.	Heth L	25
12.	1870.	Boone.........M	25
13.	1259.	Taylor. ....N	25

HENDRICKS COUNTY.
Pop. 24379 ....J   15

1.	1223.	Brown.........K	14
2.	1623	Middle..........K	14
3.	1326.	Union ....J	14
4.	1937	Eel River......J	14
5	1387	Marion ....J	15
6.	1571.	Clay...........J	15
7.	4204	Centre ....J	15
8.	2255.	Lincoln ....K	14
9.	1502	Washington ..K	15
10.	2988.	Guilford ......K	15
11.	2742.	Liberty........J	15
12	1521.	Franklin ...... J	15

HENRY COUNTY.
Pop. 23878.............Q   14

1.	862.	Blue River.....R	13
2.	2009.	Prairie... .....Q	13
3	1534.	Jefferson...... Q	13
4	2949	Fall Creek.... P	13
5.	1889	Harrison.......P	14
6.	1488	Greensboro....P	14
7.	5086.	Henry.........Q	14
8.	1834	Liberty........R	14
9.	1339.	Dudley........R	15
10.	2071	Franklin...... Q	15
11.	2803.	Spiceland.....Q	15
12.	4965.	Wayne.........P	15

HOWARD COUNTY.
Pop. 19823........... M   11

1	1000.	Jackson....... N	10
2	1697.	Liberty........N	10
3.	1707.	Howard........M	10
4.	6133.	Center........ M	10
5.	1350.	Clay L	10
6	1316	Ervin L	10
7.	1131.	Monroe........L	11
8.	893	Honey Creek .L	11
9.	807.	Harrison L	11
10.	1745.	Taylor.........M	11
11	1745.	Union..........N	11

HUNTINGTON COUNTY.
Pop. 24645............P   9

1.	2938	Jackson........Q	8
2.	1273.	Clear Creek ...Q	8
3.	951.	Warren ......P	8
4	1932.	Dallas.........P	8
5.	8091.	Huntington..;.Q	8
6	1016.	Union..........Q	8

Pop.	*Counties—continued*		
7.	1857.	Rock Creek . Q	9
8	1751.	Lancaster.... Q	9
9	960.	Polk ....P	9
10.	804.	Wayne ....P	9
11.	1227.	Jefferson ..... Q	9
12.	1813.	Salamonic.... Q	9

JACKSON COUNTY.
Pop. 20319 ... . M 20

1	1515.	Redding . .... N	19
2.	1555.	Hamilton... N	19
3.	5587.	Salt Creek... L	19
4.	1528	Owen... L	20
5	8303	Brownstown .M	20
6	1137	Jackson. ... N	20
7.	960.	Washington .N	20
8	1508	Vernon ...... N	21
9.	1158	G assy Fork .N	21
10.	922.	Driftwood ....M	21
11.	1665	Carr ... . M	21

JASPER COUNTY
Pop. 8313 ....G 7

1.	215.	Kankakee.....H	6
2.	103	Wheatfield.... G	6
3.	71.	Keener ... ... F	6
4.	281.	Walker........ G	7
5.	635.	Gillam .... H	7
6.	832.	Barkley ....G	7
7.	196	Union .... G	7
8.	468	Newton....... F	8
9.	2676.	Marion .... G	8
10	393	Hanging Grove H	8
11.	123	Milroy ....G	8
12.	327.	Jordan........ F	8
13.	1963.	Carpenter..... F	9

JAY COUNTY.
Pop. 14882............S 11

1.	933.	Wabash ....T	10
2	1247.	Bear Creek ....T	10
3.	989	Jackson........S	10
4.	1411	Penn...........S	10
5.	685.	Knox...........S	11
6.	1115.	Greene ....S	11
7.	2408.	Wayne ....T	11
8.	1218	Noble ....T	11
9.	1279	Madison .. ....T	11
10.	1595.	Pike...........T	11
11.	1640	Jefferson .... S	11
12.	1342	Richland ......R	11

JEFFERSON COUNTY.
Pop. 36102............Q 21

1.	1890	Shelby ....R	20
2	1760.	Monroe....... Q	20
3	1442.	Lancaster.....P	20
4.	1408	Graham.. .....P	21
5.	1486.	Smyrna.......P	21
6.	21352.	Madison ......Q	21
7.	1975.	Milton........R	21
8.	1973.	Hanover.......P	21
9.	1434.	Republican ...P	21

Pop.	*Counties—continued.*		
10.	1682.	Saluda ....P	22

JENNINGS COUNTY.
Pop. 16780............P 19

1	1272.	Columbia .... P	19
2	930.	Sand Creek ...P	19
3.	2037.	Geneva........O	19
4.	1927.	Spencer. ... O	20
5.	4685.	Centre ....P	19
6	1563	Campbell .....P	19
7	945.	Bigg r ....P	20
8	3315	Vernon........P	20
9.		Lovett.. ......P	20
10.	1326.	Montgomery ..P	20
11	1200.	Marion ....O	20

JOHNSON COUNTY.
Pop. 20632............M 16

1	1474	Clark . .....N	16
2.	2170	Pleasant ....M	16
3.	1755	White River .L	16
4.	1466.	Union L	17
5	5990.	Franklin .... M	17
6.	4505.	Blue River ...N	17
7	1650.	Nineveh ..... M	17
8	1668.	Hensley. L	17

KNOX COUNTY
Pop. 25137............E 21

1	2426.	Vigo.... ......F	20
2.	1704	Widner........F	20
3.	1283	Busseron .....E	20
4.	1537.	Washington ...E	21
5	1285.	Steen ....F	21
6.	1269.	Palmyra.......E	21
7.	10741	Vincennes.....D	22
8	1513	Johnson ......E	22
9.	2812	Harrison......F	22
10	837	Decker........D	22

KOSCIUSKO COUNTY.
Pop. 29256............N 6

1	1563.	Turkey Creek..O	5
2.	1899.	Van Buren....O	5
3.	711.	Jefferson .....N	5
4.	700.	Scott..........N	5
5	1415.	Etna..........M	6
6.	1248.	Prairie........N	6
7.	2239	Plain..........N	6
8.	1323	Tippecanoe....O	6
9.	3425.	Washington...O	6
10.	6349.	Wayne........N	6
11.	1745.	Harrison......N	6
12	1280	Franklin......M	7
13	1353	Seward........N	7
14	1973	Clay..........N	7
15.	990.	Monroe. ....O	7
16	1043	Jackson.......O	7
17.		Lake..........N	7

LAGRANGE COUNTY.
Pop. 16041............G 4

Pop. Counties—continued.

1.	1078	Greenfield .....R	3
2.	2067.	Lima...........Q	3
3	1347.	Van Buren ....P	3
4	1159.	Newbury.......P	3
5.	1248.	Clay ....Q	4
6.	3451.	Bloomfield.....Q	4
7	923.	Springfield.....R	4
8.	1284.	Milford........R	4
9	1322.	Johnson ......Q	4
10.	1223.	Clear Spring ..Q	4
11	930.	Eden..........P	4

LAKE COUNTY.
Pop. 12338.............E 5

1.	1593.	North..........E	4
2	1037.	Hobart.........F	4
3.	1625.	Ross...........F	5
4.	1442.	St. Johns......E	5
5.	972.	Hanover ......E	5
6	1932	Center ....E	5
7	516.	Winfield.......F	5
8	737.	Eagle Creek...F	6
9	1326.	Cedar Creek ..E	6
10.	1158.	West Creek...E	6

LA PORTE COUNTY.
Pop. 36922..............I 4

1.	636	Hudson....... .J	3
2	867.	Galena.........J	3
3.	1072.	Springfield......I	3
4.	10718.	Michigan.....H	3
5.	1328	Cool Spring....H	4
6.	1147.	Centre..........I	4
7.	10956.	Kankakee......J	4
8	884.	Wills...........J	4
9	558.	Lincoln ....J	4
10.	814.	Pleasant........J	4
11.	856.	Scipio..........I	4
12	2624.	New Durham..H	4
13.	797.	Clinton ....H	5
14.	1009.	Noble...........I	4
15.	585.	Union ....J	5
16.	170.	Johnson........J	5
17.	486.	Hanna I	5
18.	1214.	Cass...........H	5
19	202.	Dewey ....H	6

LAWRENCE COUNTY.
Pop. 18510...........K 20

1.	699.	Pleasant Run..K	20
2.	830.	Marshall........J	20
3.	982.	Perry...........J	20
4	1318	Indian Creek...J	20
5.	4765.	Shawswick.....K	20
6	967.	Flinn...........K	20
7	1292.	Guthrie........K	21
8	1005.	Bono...........K	21
9.	4693.	Marion.........K	21
10.	1939.	Spice Valley... J	21

MADISON COUNTY.
Pop. 28749.............O 13

1.	874.	Van Buren.....P	11

Pop. Counties—continued.

2.	1078.	Boone.........O	11
3.	789.	Duck Creek....N	12
4	8344.	Pipe Creek....O	12
5	2508	Monroe.......P	12
6.	1065	Richland.......P	12
7	1452	La Fayette.... O	12
8.	1344.	Jackson ....O	13
9	1178	Stony Creek...O	13
10.	7839.	Anderson ....O	13
11.	1054.	Union.........P	13
12.	1782.	Adams.........P	14
13.	3408	Fall Creek.. ..O	14
14.	1034.	Green ....N	14

MARION COUNTY.
Pop. 113679..........M 15

1.	2360	Lawrence......M	14
2.	2565.	Washington ...M	14
3	2206.	Pike L	14
4.	3738.	Wayne.........L	15
5.	4274	Centre.........M	15
6.	2567	Warren........M	15
7.	91958.	Franklin......M	15
8.	2452.	Perry..........M	15
9	1559.	Decatur.......L	15

MARSHALL COUNTY.
Pop. 24432............L 6

1.	2233	German ...... M	5
2.	1484.	North..........L	5
3.	1812	Polk...........K	5
4	1489.	West..........K	6
5.	7833.	Centre.. L	6
6.	4012.	Bourbon.......M	6
7.	1165	Tippecanoe ..M	6
8	1972.	Walnut......... L	6
9	1097.	Green L	6
10.	1335.	Union.........K	6

MARTIN COUNTY.
Pop 12867.............I 21

1	1018.	Baker...........I	20
2.	985	McCameron.. H	20
3	1048.	Brown.........H	21
4.	1026.	Mitchel Tree ..I	21
5	2176	Halbert.........I	21
6.	1170.	Center.........H	21
7.	2684	Perry.... ... H	21
8.	831.	Columbia I	22
9.	899	Lost River.....I	22
10.	1030.	Rutherford ... H	22

MIAMI COUNTY
Pop 22910...........M 9

1.	1667.	Perry..........M	8
2.	1042.	Allen..........M	8
3	982	Union..........M	8
4.	1600.	Richland......N	8
5.	1370	Jefferson ......M	9
6.	6356.	Peru..........M	9
7.	599	Erie............N	9
8.	1769.	Butler.........N	9

Pop.	*Counties—continued.*		
9.	1806.	Washington ...M	9
10	1227.	Pipe Creek....M	9
11.	1173.	Deer Creek....M	10
12.	972	Clay............M	10
13	1202.	H.rrison......N	10
14.	1645.	Jackson........N	10

MONROE COUNTY.
Pop. 17833............J 18

1	872.	Marion.........K	18
2	990.	Washington....J	18
3.	1522.	Bean Blossom.J	18
4.	2173	Richland ......J	18
5.	5632.	Bloomington .J	18
6	867.	Benton.........K	18
7.	636.	Salt Creek.....K	19
8	1513.	Perry..........J	19
9	972.	Van Buren.....J	19
10.	988.	Indian Creek...J	19
11.	1325.	Clear Creek...J	19
12.	843.	Polk..........K	19

MONTGOMERY COUNTY.
Pop 25848............H 13

1	1176.	Sugar Creek....I	12
2.	974.	Madison......H	12
3.	6429.	Coal Creek.....G	12
4	1418.	Wayne.... ...G	13
5	4875	Union . ...H	13
6	1683.	Franklin....... I	13
7	1449.	Walnut I	13
8.	1433.	Ripley.........H	14
9.	2126	Brown.........G	14
10.	1111	Scott..........H	14
11.	8174.	Clark..........I	14

MORGAN COUNTY.
Pop. 21004............K 16

1.	1042.	Madison L	16
2.	2902.	Brown.........K	16
3.	1815.	Monroe........J	16
4.	1207.	Adams.........J	16
5.	969.	Ashland.......J	16
6.	1041.	Gregg ....J	16
7.	1234.	Clay...........K	16
8.	379.	Harrison L	16
9.	1315.	Green L	16
10.	1723.	Jackson........L	17
11.	5050.	Washington....K	17
12	1081.	Jefferson...,....K	17
13	761.	Ray............J	17
14	456.	Baker.........J	17

NEWTON COUNTY.
Pop 6870............E 8

1.		Lincoln ....F	7
2	878.	Lake...........E	7
3.	141.	McClellan .... E	7
4.		Colfax........F	7
5	766.	Jackson.......F	8
6.	637.	Beaver ....E	8
7.	983.	Washington ...E	8

Pop.	*Counties—continued.*		
8.	619	Iroquois.......F	9
9.	699	Grant..........E	9
10.	2647	Jefferson......E	9

NOBLE COUNTY.
Pop. 24746...........Q 5

1	1236.	Wayne.........R	5
2.	2744	Orange.........Q	5
3	1793.	Elkhart........Q	5
4	4911.	Perry ....P	5
5	1381.	Sparta.........P	5
6.	1041.	York..........Q	5
7	3678.	Jefferson......Q	5
8.	2209.	Allen..........R	5
9	1295.	Swan..........R	6
10.	1106.	Green..........Q	6
11.	1013.	Noble..........Q	6
12.	766.	Washington...P	6
13.	1574	Albion ....Q	5

OHIO COUNTY.
Pop. 7597............T 20

1	5235	Randolph .....T	20
2.	669.	Union..........T	20
3	772	Cass ....T	20
4	921.	Pike ....S	20

ORANGE COUNTY
Pop 15315 ....J 22

1.	930.	North East ... K	22
2.	2831.	Orleans........K	21
3	904	Orangeville... J	22
4.	879.	North West... J	22
5.	1599.	French Lick ..J	22
6.	8112.	Paoli ....K	22
7.	827.	StampersCreek K	22
8.	1556.	South East.... K	23
9.	1439	Greenfield.....J	23
10.	1233.	Jackson.......J	23

OWEN COUNTY.
Pop. 18605............H 18

1.	451	Harrison.......J	17
2	757.	Taylor.........I	17
3	801	Jennings......I	17
4.	757.	Jackson.......H	17
5	1031.	Morgan........H	17
6	808.	Montgomery.. I	17
7.	2193.	Wayne........I	17
8.	4155.	Washington ...I	18
9.	1071	La Fayette....H	18
10	1767	Marion ....H	18
11.	2018.	Jefferson......H	18
12.	1512.	Franklin.......H	18
13.	1284.	Clay...........I	18

PARKE COUNTY.
Pop 20737............F 15

1.	554.	Howard........G	14
2.	878.	Sugar Creek ...F	14
3.	1540.	Liberty.... ....E	14
4.	2011.	Reserve.. .....F	14

Pop. *Counties—continued.*

5.	1614.	Penn............F	14
6.	1213.	Washington....F	14
7.	1122.	Greene.........G	15
8.	1256.	Union ....G	15
9.	4954.	Adams.........F	15
10.	781.	Wabash.........F	15
11.	2110.	Florida.........F	15
12.	1327.	Raccoon........F	15
13.	1377.	Jackson..... ..G	15

PERRY COUNTY.
Pop. 21842............J 25

1.	1440.	Oil.............J	24
2.	1567	Clark..........I	24
3.	1136.	Anderson.......I	25
4	862.	Leopold........J	25
5.	1365	Union ....J	25
6.	2566	Tobin..........J	25
7.	12906.	Troy...........I	25

PIKE COUNTY.
Pop. 11931............F 23

1.	2188.	Jefferson.......G	22
2.	8315.	Washington....F	22
3.	723.	Madison........E	22
4.	747	Clay...........E	22
5.	921.	Logan..........E	23
6.	1760.	Patoka.........F	23
7.	1428.	Marion.........G	23
8.	1829.	Lockhart.......G	24
9.	1820	Monroe.........F	24

PORTER COUNTY.
Pop. 17589..........G 5

1.	474.	Pine...........H	4
2.	1364.	Westchester ..G	4
3.	728.	Portage........F	4
4.	798.	Liberty........G	4
5.	1072.	Jackson........H	4
6.	647.	Washington.. H	5
7.	1394.	Centre.........G	5
8.	7669	Union ....F	5
9.	1006.	Porter.........G	5
10.	579.	Morgan.........G	5
11	228.	Essex..........H	5
12.	615.	Pleasant.......H	6
13.	1215.	Boone..........G	6

POSEY COUNTY.
Pop. 23385.............C 25

1.	988.	Smith..........C	24
2.	2129.	Robb. C	24
3	581.	Bethel.........B	24
4.	3067.	Harmony.......B	25
5	1666.	Lynn...........B	25
6.	955.	Centre.........C	25
7.	1683.	Robinson C	25
8.	2029.	Marr's.........C	26
9.	9957.	Black.. ....B	26
10.	980.	Point..........B	26

PULASKI COUNTY
Pop. 9849 ....I 7

Pop. *Counties—continued.*

1.	1043.	Tippecanoe ....J	7
2.	226	Franklin........J	7
3.	815.	Rich Grove....I	7
4	460.	Cass...........H	7
5.	978.	White Post ...H	7
6.	171.	Jefferson I	7
7.	2456	Monroe ....J	7
8	753.	Harrison.......J	7
9.	1175.	Van Buren.....J	8
10.	935	Indian Creek..J	8
11	489	Beaver.... I	8
12.	848.	Salem..........H	8

PUTNAM COUNTY.
Pop. 23506 ....H 15

1	1700.	Jackson I	14
2.	1266.	Franklin ..... H	14
3.	1246.	Russell........H	14
4.	1036.	Clinton........H	15
5.	1608	Monroe.........H	15
6	1269.	Floyd..........I	16
7.	1744	Marion.........I	16
8.	5335	Greencastle...H	16
9	1043	Madison ......H	16
10.	1843	Washington...H	16
11.	1601.	Warren.........H	16
12.	1080	Jefferson I	16
13	492.	Mill Creek ....J	16
14	2193.	Cloverdale I	16

RANDOLPH COUNTY.
Pop. 29590.............S 13

1	1349.	Jackson........T	12
2.	1853.	Ward ....T	12
3.	2253.	Franklin ...... S	12
4.	1243.	Green..........S	12
5.	2510	Monroe ....S	12
6	1212	Stony Creek.. R	13
7.	6196.	White River...S	13
8	5311	Wayne ....T	13
9.	2235.	Green's Fork..T	13
10	2051	Washington .. T	13
11.	1858.	West River....S	13
12.	1459.	Nettle Creek..R	13

RIPLEY COUNTY.
Pop. 21649.... ....R 19

1	2703	Adams..........S	18
2.	1874	Laughery......R	18
3.	1401.	Jackson........Q	18
4.	1531.	Centre.........R	18
5	1559.	Delaware ......R	18
6.	1961.	Franklin ......S	18
7.	1206.	Washington...S	19
8	3081	Johnson ....R	19
9	1637.	Otter Creek...Q	19
10.	2412	Shelby ....Q	20
11.	2234.	Brown ....R	20

RUSH COUNTY.
Pop. 20737...........Q 16

1	1237.	Washington ...Q	15

Pop	*Counties—continued.*
2	1615 Center.........Q 15
3	2322. Ripley.........P 15
4	1931. Posey.........P 16
5.	710. Jackson.........Q 16
6.	1206. Union.........Q 16
7.	1203 Noble.........Q 16
8	5437. Rushville.....Q 16
9	1241. Walker.........P 16
10	1273. Orange.........P 16
11.	1452 Anderson.........Q 16
12	917. Richland.........Q 16

SCOTT COUNTY.
Pop. 8990 ....O 21

1	1641 Johnson.......O 21
2.	1593. Jennings......O 21
3.	1102 Finley.........N 21
4.	1676. Vienna.........O 21
5.	2969. Lexington.....P 21

SHELBY COUNTY.
Pop. 23368..........O 16

1.	1572. Hanover........O 15
2.	1191. Van Buren ..O 15
3.	1720 Moral ....N 15
4.	1023. Sugar Creek .N 16
5.	1234. Brandywine...N 16
6.	949. Marion.........O 16
7.	1200. Union.........O 16
8.	1165. Liberty ....O 17
9.	2677 Addison.......O 17
10.	1701. Hendricks.....N 17
11.	1394. Jackson ......N 17
12	1390. Washington .O 17
13.	5851. Noble.........O 17

SPENCER COUNTY.
Pop. 20179..........H 25

1.	1977. Harrison......H 24
2.	1420. Carter.........H 24
3	426. Jackson.......G 25
4.	1385. Clay...........H 25
5	1569. Huff...........H 25
6.	2626. Hammond.....H 25
7.	1871. Grass.........G 25
8.	2381. Luce ....F 26
9.	6024. Ohio...........G 26

STARKE COUNTY.
Pop. 4667..............J 6

1.	595. Oregon.........K 5
2.	291. Davis..........J 5
3.	125 Jackson........I 6
4.	996. Center.........J 6
5	516. Washington...J 6
6.	505. North Bend...J 6
7.	251. California......J 6
8	721. Wayne.........I 6
9	637. Railroad.......H 6

STEUBEN COUNTY.
Pop. 23567............T 4

1.	455. Clear Lake.....U 3

Pop.	*Counties—continued.*
2	1562. Fremont ......T 3
3	779. Jamestown ....S 3
4	975 Mill Grove.....S 3
5.	1122 Jackson........S 4
6.	3184 Pleasant.......S 4
7.	1024 Scott..........T 4
8	857. York...........T 4
9.	653. Richland.....U 4
10.	1318 Otsego.........T 4
11.	1253 Steuben........S 4
12.	1355 Salem ....S 4

ST. JOSEPH COUNTY.
Pop 30352..........L 4

1.	408 Harris ....M 3
2.	1442 Clay...........L 3
3	551. German........L 3
4	10191. Portage.......L 4
5.	769. Warren.........K 4
6.	1560. Olive.........K 3
7.	964. Greene ....K 4
8.	714. Centre.........L 4
9	7731. Penn..........M 4
10	1697. Madison......M 4
11	1801. Union.........L 4
12	1617. Liberty.......K 4
13	1063 Lincoln.......K 4

SULLIVAN COUNTY.
Pop. 21543...... ... .F 19

1.	1732. Jackson ......F 18
2.	2171. Curry ....E 18
3.	1234. Fairbanks ...D 18
4.	1933 Turman ....D 19
5.	5672. Hamilton .....E 19
6	1488 Cass...........F 19
7.	1251 Jefferson......F 20
8.	3491. Haddon ....E 20
9	2561. Gill ....D 19

SWITZERLAND COUNTY.
Pop. 14321...........S 21

1	2183. Posey ....T 20
2.	995. York...........T 21
3.	1700 Colton ....S 20
4.	5155 Jefferson......S 21
5	2145. Pleasant.......S 21
6.	1843. Craig ....S 21

TIPPECANOE COUNTY.
Pop. 49244...........H 11

1.	1724. Washington....I 10
2	2271. Tippecanoe....H 10
3.	2129 Wabash........H 11
4.	1395. Shelby.........G 10
5	8345. Fairfield.......H 11
6.	1491 Perry..........I 11
7.	1954. Sheffield......I 11
8	1251. Wea...........H 11
	Union...........H 11
10	2134 Wayne.........G 11
11.	19258. Jackson ....G 12
12.	1032. Randolph.....H 12

Pop. *Counties—continued.*

13. 8237. Lauramie.......I 12

TIPTON COUNTY.
Pop. 13294...........M 12

1.	1547.	Wildcat......N	11
2.	1746.	Liberty.......M	11
3.	1547.	Prairie........L	11
4.	1739	Jefferson......L	12
5.	4987	Cicero.........M	12
6.	1729.	Madison......N	12

UNION COUNTY.
Pop. 7859.............T 16

1.	759.	Harrison......T	15
2.	1853.	Brownsville.. T	15
3.	763.	Liberty........T	16
4	2961	Centre.........T	16
5	734.	Harmony......T	16
6.	1289.	Union.........T	16

VANDERBURGH COUNTY.
Pop. 48830...........D 25

1.	1677	Scott..........D	25
2.	1290.	Armstrong ....D	25
3.	1683	German.......D	25
4.	89201	Center........D	25
5.	1342	Knight........E	25
6.	875.	Pigeon ....D	25
7.	1719	Perry.........D	26
8.	1040	Union.........D	26

VERMILLION COUNTY.
Pop. 13212.............E 14

1.	2984	Highland......E	13
2.	1743.	Eugene.......E	14
3.	2773.	Vermillion....E	14
4.	2794	Helt...........E	15
5.	2913	Clinton ....E	16

VIGO COUNTY.
Pop. 33749............E 17

1.	1299.	Nevins........F	16
2	1269.	Otter Creek ...F	16
3.	1912.	Fayette.......E	16
4.	23357.	Sugar Creek...E	17
5.	870.	Harrison ......E	17
6.	1914.	Lost Creek....F	17
7.	1492.	Riley..........F	17
8.	1519.	Honey Creek..E	17
9.	955.	Prairieton.....E	17
10	1236.	Prairie Creek..D	18
11.	1437.	Linton........E	18
12.	1489.	Pierson ....F	18

WABASH COUNTY.
Pop. 23007...........O 8

1.	8148.	Chester........O	8
2.	5958.	Pleasant.......N	8
3.		Paw Paw......N	8
4.	4485	Noble.........N	9
5.	4879.	Lagro.........O	9

Pop. *Counties—continued.*

6.	1816.	Liberty........O	9
7.	2732	Waltz.........N	9

WARREN COUNTY.
Pop. 11375...........F 11

1.	609.	Medina........G	11
2.	809.	J. Q. Adams...F	11
3.	1032.	Pine..........F	11
4.	667.	Prairie........E	11
5.	448.	Jordan........E	11
6.	1176.	Liberty ....F	11
7.	1391.	Warren.......F	11
8.	2239.	Washington .. F	12
9.	941.	Pike..........E	12
10.	1068.	Steuben.......E	12
11.	601.	Kent..........E	12
12.	894	Mound........E	13

WARRICK COUNTY.
Pop. 21493 ....F 25

1.	1646	Pigeon.........G	24
2.	870.	Lane ....F	24
3	1440.	Owen ....F	24
4.	1892.	Hart...........F	24
5.	864	Greer.........E	24
6.	1437.	Campbell ......E	25
7.	5776.	Boone.........F	25
8.	1330.	Skelton........G	25
9.	5396.	Ohio ....E	25
10.	842.	Anderson......F	26

WASHINGTON COUNTY.
Pop. 20531...........M 22

1.	1525.	Gibson........ N	21
2.	1059.	Monroe...... . M	21
3.	1532.	Jefferson L	21
4.	1521.	Brown L	21
5.	1101.	Vernon L	22
6.	5711	Washington.. M	22
7.	1366.	Franklin .....N	22
8.	920.	Polk ....N	22
9.	1179.	Pierce.........M	22
10.	1159.	Howard........L	22
11.	835.	Madison.......L	22
12.	1722.	Posey.........L	23
13.	902.	Jackson.......M	23

WAYNE COUNTY.
Pop. 46039............S 14

1.	1697.	Franklin.......T	14
2.	1893.	New Garden ..T	14
3.	1541.	Green.........S	14
4.	13889.	Perry.........S	14
5.	839.	Dalton........R	14
6.	2829.	Jefferson......S	14
7.	9017.	Jackson ....R	15
8	580.	Harrison.......S	14
9.	1547	Clay ....S	14
10		Webster.......T	14
11	8932.	Centre .. ..T	15
12.	8731.	Wayne.........T	15
13.	894.	Boston........T	15

Pop.	Counties—continued.		
14.	591.	Abington.......T	15
15.	2863	Washington....S	15

WELLS COUNTY.
Pop. 15238..........R 9

1	1773.	Jefferson.......S	8
2.	1263.	Union.......R	8
3.	1326.	Rock Creek...R	9
4.	1391.	Lancaster .... S	9
5.	4614.	Harrison ......S	9
6.	1097.	Liberty ....R	9
7.	1140.	Jackson........Q	10
8.	1212.	Chester ....R	10
9.	1432.	Nottingham ..S	10

WHITE COUNTY.
Pop. 13095.......... H 9

1.	451.	Cass ....J	8
2	838.	Liberty.........I	8
3.	1165.	Monon.........H	8
4	960.	Princeton .....G	9
5.	937.	Honey Creek..H	9
6.	2719.	Union I	9
7.	1825.	Jackson........J	9
8	594.	Big Creek.....H	9
9.	611.	West Point ...H	9
10	401.	Round Grove.G	10
11.	2553	Prairie........H	10

WHITLEY COUNTY.
Pop. 15175...........P 7

1	1232	Smith..... ....Q	6
2.	1343.	Thorn Creek..Q	6
3.	429.	Etna ....P	6
4.	894.	Troy ....P	6
5	1723.	Richland......P	7
6.	8518.	Columbia......P	7
7.	1486.	Union .... Q	7
8.	1263.	Jefferson......Q	7
9.	1246.	Washington...P	7
10.	2041.	Cleveland......P	7

LAKES.

Beaver...................E	7
Cedar..................J	6
English..................I	6
James ....S	4
Manitau L	7
Maxinkuckee..........K	6
Mill Pond..............Q	5
Mud....................J	4
Tippecanoe ....O	6
Turkey.................P	5
Wawasee . ...O	5

RIVERS.

Alleman's Creek ....G	22
Bean Blossom Creek.....K	18

Rivers—continued.	
Beaver Creek.............I	21
Big Blue.................P	15
Big Creek.................H	9
Big Creek................B	25
Big Melamonong Creek...I	8
Big Raccoon Creek.......F	15
Big Slough...............G	8
Black Creek..............Q	10
Blue L	23
Blue Creek...............T	19
Buck Creek..............M	25
Busseron Creek..........E	20
Carpenter Creck.........F	9
Cicero Creek..............L	12
Clear Creek..............P	8
Coal Creek ....E	14
Deer Creek..............H	16
Deer Creek..............K	10
Duck Creek......... ... N	13
Eagle....................L	14
East Fork White River...I	21
Eel......................G	17
Eel......................M	8
Elkhart..................N	3
Fall Creek...............N	14
Furse Creek.............H	19
Graham Fork............P	20
Honey Creek.............H	9
Indian Creek.............L	24
Indian Creek.............I	19
Iroquois.................E	9
Kankakee...............E	7
Laughery Creek.........R	19
Lick Creek..............J	22
Lick Creek..............Q	11
Little Blue...............P	15
Little Monon Creek.....H	9
Little Pigeon Creek.....F	26
Lost....................I	22
Lugar's Creek...........P	10
Martindale Creek........S	14
Maumee................S	7
Mill Creek...............J	7
Mississinneua ....P	11
Moore's Creek..........H	10
Mud Creek..............L	7
Muddy Creek...........L	19
Muscatatuck...........M	21
North Fork...............L	5
North Fork Salt Creek...L	18
Ohio....................M	25
Patoka..................D	23
Pickamink..............G	8
Pigeon ....Q	4
Pine Creek..............F	11
Pine Creek..............N	4
Pipe Creek..............M	10
Prairie Creek............D	18
Prairie Creek ....F	21
Rock Creek.............P	9
Rock Creek.............K	10
Salamonie...............O	9
Salt Creek...............J	20
Sand Creek..............P	19

Pop.	Towns—continued.		
25.	Braysville..........I		18
	Braysville, see		
	New Trenton....T		18
50.	Brasto wn ....S		21
2745.	Brazil..............G		16
906.	Bremen.............M		5
25.	Brentsville, 2 m N		
	E Spencer........I		18
160.	Bretzville.... ...JL		24
50.	Brewersville.......P		19
	Briant, see Bryant.T		10
25	Brick Chapel......H		15
15.	Bridgeport, 11 m		
	N W Leopold....J		25
30.	Bridgeport ....N		24
25.	Bridgeport.........L		15
	Bridgeport, see		
	Adyeville........ I		24
101	Bridgeton......... F		16
25.	Bright.............T		18
29.	Brighton. .....R		3
15.	Brights, 2 m N W		
	Wirt..............Q		21
25.	Brightwood.......M		15
207.	Brimfield ....Q		5
240.	Bringhurst........ J		10
513.	Bristol.............O		3
25.	Bristow............I		25
	Brittons, see New		
	Britton..........M		11
25.	Broad Ripple, 6 m		
	N Indianapolis..M		15
	Brockman Cross		
	Roads, see Edin-		
	burgh............N		17
	Brockman, see Ed-		
	inburgh..........N		17
25.	Brockville, 3 m N		
	Angola ....T		4
100.	Brook ....E		8
50.	Brookfield........N		16
181.	Brooklyn..........K		16
25.	Brooksburgh......R		21
555.	Brookston........H		10
2178.	Brookville........T		17
20	Broom Hill........N		23
	Browns, see Indi-		
	anapolis ....M		15
753.	Brownsburgh .....K		14
135.	Brown's Corners..Q		9
	Browntown, sub-		
	urb Logansport.K		9
723	Brownstown ....M		20
25.	Brownstown Sta-		
	tion..............M		20
15.	Brownville, 3 m N		
	E Hartford......E		18
453.	Brownsville ....T		15
	Brownsville, see		
	Brown's Valley..H		14
75.	Brown's Valley...H		14
120	Bruceville........E		21
30	Bruce's, 3 m S W		
	Cedar Lake......S		6

Pop.	Towns—continued.		
25.	Bruce's Lake, 12		
	m N E Star City.J		8
25.	Brunerstown ......G		16
100.	Brunswick.........E		5
75.	Brushy Prairie....R		4
100.	Bryant ....T		10
38.	Bryantsburgh......Q		20
25.	Bryant's Creek....J		17
35.	Bryantsville ......J		21
25.	Buchanan ....N		24
15	Buck Creek.......I		11
25.	Buckskin ....E		24
20.	Buena Vista.......I		19
25.	Buena Vista.......N		25
25.	Buena Vista, 3 m N		
	E Winamac......J		7
100.	Buena Vista........S		13
207.	Buena Vista...... M		12
50	Buena Vista ....S		10
30.	Buena Vista.. ....R		17
	Buena Vista, see		
	Six Mile Post, 7		
	m W Vernon....P		19
20	Buffalo............M		19
25.	Buffaloville....... H		25
	Bugtown, see Win-		
	field, 16 m N Mt.		
	Vernon ....B		26
	Bull Creek, see		
	Herculaneum, 6		
	m N Charles-		
	town.............O		23
28.	Bull Rapids, 15 m E		
	Ft. Wayne........S		7
165.	Bunker Hill.......M		10
25.	Bunker Hill, 5 m		
	N W Conners-		
	ville..............R		16
15.	Bunkum ....T		18
25.	Burdick ....H		4
30.	Burget Corner....L		12
195.	Burlington ....K		11
30.	Burlington, 9 m W		
	Rushville........Q		16
60.	Burnett, 7 m N E		
	Terre Haute .... E		17
227.	Burnett's Creek....J		9
25.	Burnettsville .....J		9
15.	Burnside .... K		11
20	Burnside ....N		16
75.	Burnsville........O		18
105.	Burrows...........J		9
25	Busaco, 2 m N		
	Denver..........M		8
35.	Busseron........... E		20
948.	Butler.............T		5
	Butlers, see But-		
	ler's Switch......P		20
25.	Butler's Switch...P		20
193.	Butlerville........P		19
15.	Byron, 8 m N E La-		
	porte I		4
25	Buzroen's Mill, 4 m		
	N E Sullivan ... E		19

Pop	Towns—continued.		
	Glen Heron, see		
	Connersville	S	16
24.	Glenn Valley......	L	16
100.	Glenwood......	R	16
25.	Goddard's.........	P	16
30.	Goldsmith	M	12
888.	Goodland...	F	9
25	Goodwin's Cor-		
	ners .... S .	T	16
16.	Goshen, 3 m S E		
	Scottsburg......	O	21
8759.	Goshen.............	O	4
736.	Gosport.........	I	17
25	Gooseport.........	N	21
34.	Grafton..........	B	25
20	Graham	P	21
15.	Graham, 5 m S E		
	Butlersville......	P	19
25.	Grand Crossing, 6		
	m S E Avilla.. .	R	5
67.	Grand Rapids		
	Crossing.........	R	6
839.	Grandview........	H	26
25	Granger..........	M	3
30.	Grant.	F	16
15.	Grant, 4 m W		
	Akron..	M	7
50.	Grant City	P	14
50.	Grantsburg	K	24
25.	Grants Creek, 8 m		
	N E Florence...	T	21
50.	Granville.........	R	12
15.	Grassy Valley, 10 m		
	S W Corydon....	M	24
25.	Gravel Pit.........	E	17
29	Gravel Pit.........	H	11
87.	Gravel Pit.........	O	13
35	Gravel Pit.........	N	25
30	Gravel Pit.........	E	12
15.	Gravel Pit	O	6
	Gravel Point, see		
	Gravel Pit.......	N	25
20	Gravelton, 4 m W		
	Milford..........	N	5
	*Gravelton, Fulton		
	Co.		
25	Gray's Pan Yard,		
	10 m S E Clear		
	Creek.	J	19
28.	Graysville.........	O	23
60	Graysville.........	D	19
30	Green Brier......	J	23
3673.	Greencastle........	H	16
25.	Green Centre......	Q	6
	Greendale, see Law-		
	renceburgh......	T	19
37.	Greene	S	11
1881	Greenfield	O	15
25	Greenfield Mills, 14		
	m N E LaGrange.	Q	4
	Green Fork, see		
	Washington.....	S	14
255.	Green Hill, 18 m N		
	E Williamsport..	F	12

Pop.	Towns—continued.		
25.	Green Oak........	L	7
424.	Greensborough....	Q	14
3513	Greensburgh.......	Q	17
25.	Green's Fork, 9 m		
	N W Richmond..	T	14
294	Greenville..... ...	M	23
270.	Greentown, 8 m E		
	Kokomo..........	M	10
70.	Greentown.........	N	11
25.	Greenwood........	S	8
696.	Greenwood........	N	16
15.	Greetingsville, 9 m		
	N E Frankfort....	J	12
20.	Griffen Station, 6		
	m E Rushville....	Q	16
25.	Griffins............	Q	16
30.	Grisby's...........	G	25
28.	Grismore..........	P	5
25.	Griswold...........	E	20
30.	Groomsville	L	11
67.	Groveland..........	I	15
85.	Grovertown........	J	5
25.	Groves, 8 m N W		
	Connersville	S	16
100.	Guilford............	T	18
20	Guionsville	S	20
25.	Gundrum..........	I	7
15.	Guthrie.......	J	19
	Gwynne's, see		
	Gwynne's Mills...	P	16
30.	Gwynne's Mills....	P	16
25.	Hackleman........	O	11
65	Hackman's Cross		
	Roads, 2 m S W		
	Batesville..	R	18
24.	Hadley............	J	15
20.	Hadley	R	7
28.	Hageman..........	G	4
1048.	Hagerstown.	S	14
	Halberts Bluff, see		
	Shoals............	I	21
25	Haley.............	T	14
	Half Way, see Red		
	Key..............	S	11
60.	Hall..............	J	16
20	Hall's Corners.....	T	6
27.	Hamburg..........	R	17
25.	Hamburg, 1 m S W		
	Sellersburg	O	23
15.	Hamers Mill, 3 m		
	N E Mitchell....	K	21
135	Hamilton..........	T	4
25.	Hamilton..........	L	14
29	Hamilton	J	11
25.	Hamilton..........	S	6
30.	Hamilton..........	O	13
20.	Hamilton Station..	J	12
50	Hamlet............	J	5
25.	Hammoud..........	D	4
20.	Hampton, 3 m E		
	Danville..........	J	15
30.	Hamrick's.........	H	16
	Hamrick's Station,		
	see Hamrick's...	H	16

Pop.	Towns—continued.			Pop.	Towns—continued.		
25.	Lancaster........	P	20	340	Lexington	P	22
30.	Lancaster. 11 m S			30.	Lexington........	J	11
	E Vernon	P	19	60.	Lexington	R	3
20.	Lancaster	K	21	65	Liber............	T	11
175.	Lancaster, 4 m S				Liberty, see North		
	Huntington.....	P	8		Liberty	K	4
25	Lancaster.........	H	18	20.	Liberty, 3 m S W		
100.	Lancaster........	R	9		Bedford	J	20
27.	Lancaster........	T	11	1055.	Liberty..........	T	16
30.	Landersdale......	L	16	25.	Liberty, 3 m S W		
25	Lane.............	H	13		Franklin	M	17
363	Lanesville.......	M	24	25	Liberty..........	T	8
20	Lanesville, 2 m N			30	Liberty Centre, 4		
	E Indianapolis..M		15		m S W Bluffton..R		9
30.	Langdon's... ...N		20	211	Liberty Mills......O		7
15.	Lansing. 5 m N			20.	Libertyville ......D		16
	Dyer............D		5	15.	Lick Creek........J		22
25.	La Otto...........R		6	1776.	Ligonier ....P		5
100	La Paz L		5	25	Lilydale...........J		25
9771.	La Porte..........I		4	419.	Lima ....Q		3
25.	Lardona, 3 m W				Limber List, see		
	Morristown .....O		15		Geneva ....T		10
30.	Larenture, 5 m E			30.	Limedale...........H		16
	Ft. Wayne.......S		7	25	Lincoln...........H		25
395.	Larwill ....P		6	175.	Lincoln L		10
35.	Laud ....Q		7	150.	Lincoln...........M		8
20.	Laughery Switch..R		19	20.	Lincoln City, see		
25.	Laugheryville....R		18		Lincoln........H		25
30.	Laughter, 4 m N E			180.	Lincolnville ......O		9
	Versailles....... R		19	25.	Lincolnville......R		19
1122.	Laurel ....R		16	167.	Linden ....H		12
60.	Lawrence.........M		14		Linden Hill, see		
25.	Lawrence.........S		5		Richmond......T		14
4881.	Lawrenceburgh...T		19	145.	Linksville, 5 m N		
37.	Lawrenceport.....K		21		E Plymouth L		6
25.	Lawrenceville....S		18	208	Linn Grove........S		10
20.	Lawrenceville, 10			175.	Linton ....F		19
	m N W Guilford.T		18	1095.	Linwood, suburb		
15.	Layne's Mills......I		16		of Lafayette....H		11
25.	Leamon Corner...O		14	90.	Lisbon............R		5
699	Leavenworth......K		24	25.	Liston, 9 m S W		
2586.	Lebanon..........K		13		Wabash........O		9
25.	Lee, 6 m W Boon-			15	Little Point.......J		16
	ville.............F		25	87.	Little York........N		21
541	Leesburgh.... ...N		6	25.	Liverpool.........F		4
155.	Leesville..........L		20	284	Livonia L		22
20	Leipsic...:........K		21	120.	Lizton............J		14
15.	Leiter's Ford......K		7	207.	Locke ....M		5
90.	Lena ....G		16	25.	Lockport ....S		15
240	Leo...............S		6	40	Lockport ....F		17
20	Leonida...........M		9	20.	Lockport. ....J		9
27.	Leopold...,.......J		25	15.	Lockport, 3 m W		
25.	Leoti.............G		24		Cory..........F		17
30	Le Roy...........F		5	60.	Lock Spring.......Q		19
28	Lett's Corner.....P		18	18.	Locust Point, 3 m		
25.	Lettsville.........F		21		S Corydon.......M		24
20	Lewis ....F		18	25	Lodi..............E		14
30.	Lewisburg........R		7	15.	Lodi, 3 m S W		
15.	Lewisburg, 3 m N				County Line.....N		7
	Greenfield .... O		15	65.	Lodi..............F		16
25.	Lewisburgh.......L		9		Logan, see Logan		
30.	Lewis Creek......N		17		Cross Roads......T		18
494	Lewisville ....Q		15	25.	Logan CrossRoads.T		18
25	Lewisville.........J		17	11364.	Logansport........K		9

Pop.	Towns—continued.		
25.	Maxinkuckee	K	6
60.	MaxinkuckeeLake	K	6
	Maxville, see		
	Macksville	S	13
60	Maxville, 15 m N E		
	Rockport	G	26
275.	Maysville	T	6
20.	Maysville, 2 m W		
	Washington	F	21
80.	Maysville, 8 m S E		
	Huntington	P	8
25	Maywood	L	15
	Mecca, see Mecca		
	Mills	F	15
85.	Mecca Mills	F	15
225.	Mechanicsburgh	P	13
90.	Mechanicsburgh	J	13
15.	Mecha icsburgh,		
	3 m N W Indian-		
	apolis	M	15
25.	Mechanicsville	D	25
200.	Medaryaville	H	7
298	Medora	L	20
20.	Melissaville	R	18
50	Memphis	O	22
25	Mercury	O	12
537.	Merom	D	19
30	Merriam, 8 m S		
	Albion	Q	5
125.	Merrillville	F	5
33 l.	Metamora	S	17
25	Metea	L	8
375.	Metz	U	4
250.	Mexico	M	9
75.	Miami	N	10
25.	Michigan Central		
	Junction	G	4
6030.	Michigan City	H	3
200.	Michigantown	K	11
25.	Middleborough	U	14
125	Middlebury	G	18
543	Middlebury	O	3
	Middlebury Station,		
	see Vistula, 5 m		
	N E Bristol	O	3
20.	Middle Fork	Q	20
75.	Middle Fork	K	11
25	Middleton	L	11
696.	Middletown	P	13
20	Middletown, 1 m S		
	E Quincy	I	17
75.	Middletown	P	17
	Middletown, see		
	Wesley	G	13
25.	Middletown	H	18
40.	Middletown	E	18
23.	Middletown	S	8
20.	Midway	H	18
80.	Midway	G	25
15.	Midway, 1 m S W		
	Colfax	J	12
107.	Mier	O	10
37.	Mifflin	J	23
225.	Milan	S	19

Pop.	Towns—continued.		
432.	Milford	N	5
25	Milford	G	11
531.	Milford	P	17
15	Milford Junction	N	5
80.	Mill Ark, 7 m S E		
	Rochester	L	7
25.	Millarsville	M	14
18.	Mill Creek, 10 m E		
	La Porte	I	4
20.	Milledgeville	K	14
15.	Miller, 2 m N Law-		
	renceburgh	T	19
30.	Millers	D	23
27.	Millers	F	4
	Millers, see Mil-		
	lersburgh	M	12
15.	Millers, 8 m N		
	Rochester	L	7
	Millers Corners,		
	see Milners Cor-		
	ners	O	14
30.	Millers	G	25
20.	Millers, 8 m N W		
	Indianapolis	M	15
25	Millersburgh	K	22
30	Millersburgh, 5 m		
	S W Versailles	R	19
25.	Millersburgh	K	22
15	Millersburgh	M	13
630.	Millersburgh	P	7
18.	Millersburgh	O	4
28.	Millersburgh	E	25
15	Miller Station	L	7
25.	Millersport	G	23
	Miller's Station,		
	see Millers	F	4
75.	Mill Grove	R	11
20.	Mill Grove, 1 m N		
	W Quincy	I	17
150.	Millhousen	Q	18
	Millingeville, see		
	Milledgeville	K	14
25.	Millport	M	21
25	Mills Corners	S	10
30.	Mill Switch	O	12
84.	Milltown	L	23
175.	Millville	R	14
25	Millwood	M	5
30.	Milners Corners	O	14
209.	Milroy	Q	16
15.	Milton	F	16
30	Milton	S	20
974.	Milton	S	15
25.	Mineral City	H	19
2802	Mishawaka	L	4
25.	Mishawaka, 4 m N		
	South Bend	L	4
1677.	Mitchell	K	21
75.	Mixersville	U	16
25	Monan Mills, 8 m		
	E Bradford	H	8
225.	Mongo	R	3
80.	Mongoquinong, 8		
	m N E La Grange	Q	4

Pop.	Towns—continued.			P. p.	Towns—continued.		
100.	Monitor	I	11	261.	Mount Etna	P	9
25.	Monmouth	T	8	25.	Mount Etna, 2 m N		
30.	Monon	H	8		Rushville	Q	16
15.	Monong, 2 m E			21.	Mount Gilboa, 3 m		
	Bradford	H	8		E Earl Park	E	9
20.	Monoquet	N	6	18.	Mount Healthy	M	19
25.	Monroe	I	12	30.	Mount Hope	T	5
40.	Monroe	T	9	75.	Mount Jack on	M	15
	Monroe Centre,			25.	Mount Jefferson	M	15
	see Monroe	T	9	21.	Mount Liberty, 6		
227.	Monroe City	E	22		m S E Nashville	L	18
28.	Monroe Mills	K	17	135.	Mount Meridian	I	16
1089.	Monroeville	T	8	25.	Mount Moriah	M	18
306.	Monrovia	J	16	15.	Mount Nebo, 3 m		
210.	Monterey	J	7		N E Earl Park	E	9
25.	Montez, 6 m S W			27.	Mount Pisgah	R	4
	Logansport	K	9	23.	Mount Prospect	J	23
657.	Montezuma	E	15	18.	Mount Pleasant	R	13
369.	Montgomery	G	21	30.	Mount Pleasant	J	25
21.	Montgomery, 7 m			15.	Mount Pleasant, 2		
	N E Cana	O	20		m N Indian-		
	Montgomery Sta-				apolis	M	15
	tion, see Mont-			25.	Mount Pleasant	H	21
	gomery	G	21	30.	Mount Pleasant	O	17
999.	Monticello	I	9	18.	Mount Sidney	N	21
30.	Montmorency	G	11	40.	Mount Sterling	S	21
615.	Montpelier	R	10	225.	Mount Summit	Q	13
	*Monument City,			25.	Mount Tabor	J	17
	Huntington Co.			30.	Mount Vernon	O	10
25.	Mooney	L	20	25.	Mount Vernon	L	8
40.	Moorefield	S	21	3676.	Mount Vernon	B	26
23.	Moorehouse	N	3	18.	Mount Zion	R	10
20.	Mooresburgh, 6 m			15.	Mowea, 4 m N E		
	S E Winamac	J	7		Flat Rock	N	17
657.	Moores Hill	S	19	30.	Muddy Fork	N	23
18.	Mooretown	J	21	25.	Mud Lick	Q	20
	Moores Station,			125.	Mulberry	I	11
	see Mooresville	T	5	4515.	Muncie	Q	12
25.	Mooresville	T	5	25.	Munday's	I	17
969.	Mooresville	K	16	15.	Mundy Station, 5 m		
228.	Mooresville	O	23		N E Spencer	I	18
25.	Moore's Vineyard	M	18	28.	Murphy, 2 m S		
30.	Moral	N	15		Memphis	O	22
75.	Moran	J	11	30.	Murray	R	9
25.	Morehouse, 4 m W			25.	Murray Road	R	9
	Julietta	N	15	20.	Murrys Mills, 2 m		
30.	Morgan	I	5		S E Rising Sun	T	20
275.	Morgantown	L	17	15.	Muscamtuck, 6 m		
184.	Morocco	E	8		N W Browns-		
318.	Morris	R	18		town	M	20
453.	Morristown	O	15		Musselman, see		
110.	Morristown	S	12		Newburgh	E	26
25.	Morton	H	15	30.	Nabb's	P	22
	Mortonsville, sub-			325.	Napoleon	R	18
	urb of Delphi	J	10	255.	Nappanee	N	5
30.	Morvan	L	25	25.	Nash Depot	D	24
125.	Moscow	P	17	15.	Nashua, 12 m N		
25.	Mound City	E	13		Evansville	D	25
33.	Mountain Spring	I	20	27.	Nashville	P	14
76.	Mount Auburn	N	17	435.	Nashville	L	18
25.	Mount Cameron	H	20		Nashville, see Love-		
18.	Mount Carmel	L	21		ly Dale, 10 m S E		
152.	Mount Carmel	T	17		Vincennes	D	21
87.	Mount Comfort	N	15	25.	Natchez	I	22

Pop.	Towns—continued.		
100.	New Providence...N	23
45.	New Richmond....H	12
187.	New Ross............I	14
25.	New Salem.........Q	16
33.	New Salisbury.....M	23
25.	Newton's Retreat.H	11
75.	Newton Stewart .J	23
165.	Newtonville.......H	25
195.	Newtown...........G	12
25.	Newtown...........T	19
100.	New Trenton......T	18
25.	Newry.............O	20
307.	Newville............T	5
25.	Newville, 2 m S E	
	Blufftcn..........R	9
140.	New Washington..P	22
100.	New Waverly......L	9
175.	New Winchester.. J	15
30.	Nickolsonville, 3 m	
	N E Noblesville.M	13
20.	Niconza............N	8
15.	Nine Mile...... .R	8
25.	Nineveh ....M	17
	Nixon, see New	
	Castle............Q	14
18.	Noah...............O	16
30.	Noblesville ....Q	6
	Noble, see Nobles-	
	ville ....Q	6
2184.	Noblesville........M	13
25.	Nora...............J	15
35.	Nora...............M	14
75.	Normanda.........L	12
50.	Norristown........O	17
25.	North, 2 m S Celes-	
	tine I	23
15.	North Bend, 13 m S	
	North Judson.....I	6
20.	North Belleville....J	15
	North Benton, see	
	Benton............S	4
	North Boston, see	
	New Boston.......I	25
	North Branch, see	
	Brazil............G	16
	North Bridgeport,	
	see Bridgeport...L	15
25.	Northern Depot...K	13
37.	Northfield. L	13
	North Fillmore,see	
	Fillmore..........I	15
50.	North Galveston, 8	
	m N W Warsaw..N	6
97.	North Grove.......N	10
25.	North Hogan.......S	18
20.	North Indianapolis L	15
180.	North Judson.......I	6
	North Landing,see	
	North's Landing.T	20
50.	North's Landing...T	20
800.	North Liberty.....K	4
75.	North Madison....Q	21
25.	Northport, 1 m N	
	Rome City........Q	5

Pop.	Towns—continued.		
1260.	North Manchester.O	7
25.	North Salem, 3 m S	
	E Plymouth......L	5
100.	North Salem.......J	14
30.	North Shops, 4 m S	
	Peru..............M	9
25.	North Street, 1 m N	
	Indianapolis.....M	15
50	North Union......H	14
2034	North Vernon.... .P	19
25.	North Vernon, 3 m	
	S E Brookville....T	17
50	Norway............I	9
30	North Williams-	
	burgh,3 m W Dan-	
	ville.......... ....J	15
	*No Town, Jasper Co.	
75	Notre Dame.......L	3
25	Nottingham...... .S	10
	Null's Mills, ace	
	Nulltown........S	16
35	Nulltown...........S	16
25.	Numa..............E	16
40.	Nyesville..........F	15
40.	Oak... .....•......J	8
30.	Oakalla ....H	16
25.	Oakdale ....P	19
25.	Oakdam............E	24
80	Oak Farm..........L	18
75.	Oakford. ....M	11
25.	Oak Forest........S	17
	Oakland, see Oak-	
	landon...........N	14
30.	Oakland I	16
15	Oakland ....G	25
96.	Oakland City......E	23
40.	Oaklandon........N	14
25.	Oak Plain........K	15
30.	Oak Ridge.........M	6
147	Oaktown..........E	20
25	Oakville, 8 m S	
	Muncie............Q	12
28	Oakwood, 6 m E	
	Marion............P	10
	Oceola, see Osce-	
	ola................M	4
23.	Octagon...........H	10
40.	Odell..............G	12
200.	Ogden.............Q	15
25.	Ohio...........•....F	13
47.	Oil Creek..........J	24
1259.	Oldenburgh........R	17
25.	Old Indian Village O	10
193.	Olean ....R	19
30.	Olio................N	14
20.	Olive Hill,6 m N W	
	Richmond........T	14
15.	Oloosa, 12 m N W	
	Medarysville....H	7
25.	Omega.............M	12
28.	One Forty Six.....N	9
80	Oneida, 10 m S	
	Warsaw...........N	6
30.	One Sixty One L	9

Pop.	Towns—continued.	
25.	Rock Lick, 12 m S E Corjdon.....M	24
2187.	Rockport ....G	26
25.	Rockport Mills, 8 m N W Rockville F	15
1666.	Rockville.........F	15
80.	Roet, 5 m S E Ft. Wayne........S	7
23.	Rogersville........R	13
250.	Rolling Prairie....J	3
275.	Rome.............J	26
300.	Rome City.......Q	5
25.	Rome Station.....Q	5
150.	Romney ... .H	12
80.	Rono.............K	25
18	Root..............S	8
25.	Roseburgh........T	16
20	Roseburgh.........O	10
15.	Rose Creek........J	19
125.	Rosedale.........F	16
25.	Rosedale..........J	8
80.	Rosehill..........O	7
94.	Roseville.........F	16
28.	Rosewood .. ..N	25
25.	Ross.............E	4
15.	Rossburg, 3 m E Greensburgh.....Q	17
	Ross Station, see Ross ....E	4
80.	Rossville........R	17
516.	Rossville.........J	11
200.	Royal Centre.....K	8
25.	Royalton..........K	14
159.	Royerton.........Q	12
20.	Rozelle, 3 m N La Crosse.........H	6
80.	Ruddle's Addition.O	13
15.	Runcorn, 1 m W Washington......F	21
25.	Rumbargers......J	17
	Rumbargers Station,see Rumbargers ....J	17
25.	Rural...........T	13
80.	Rushawn, 6 m N W La Grange.......Q	4
25.	Rush Creek.......L	21
	Rush Creek Valley, see Rush Creek..L	21
2160	Rushville.........Q	16
25.	Russel, 3 m N E Knox...........J	6
28.	Russells Mills......F	14
90.	Russellville.......H	14
225.	Russiaville.......L	11
	Ryantsburgh, see B yant burgh....Q	20
25.	Rynear..... ......F	18
20.	Sabine..........L	15
147.	Salamonia.... ...T	11
83.	Salem............T	13
	Salem, see Jordan, 12 m S E PortlandT	11
1533.	Salem.............M	22

Pop.	Towns—continued.	
25.	Salem............T	9
28.	Salem.. ....F	8
90.	Salem Centre.....S	4
	Salem Crossing,see Otis ....H	4
23.	Salina...........L	7
80.	Salina............N	24
45.	Saline City........G	17
	Salisbury, see New Salisbury.......M	23
25.	Salisbury.........I	19
35.	Salmon, 4 m S E Brookville........T	17
25.	Salt Creek .. ..J	20
20.	Salt Creek........G	4
15.	Saltillo, 10 m N E Rensselaer......G	8
200.	Saltillo............L	21
	Saltilloville, see Saltillo............L	21
25.	Saluda ....Q	21
80.	Samaria.........L	17
40.	Sandborn ......F	20
25.	Sand Creek .....F	15
20.	Sand Cut, 3 m S Rosedale ....F	16
15.	Sand Pit.........J	20
100.	Sanford...........D	16
80.	Sandsburgh, 6 m N W Spencer........I	18
25.	San Jacinto.......Q	20
185.	San Pierre........H	6
25.	Santa Claus.......H	25
90.	Santa Fe........N	10
80.	Santa Fe............I	17
15.	Santa Fe..........H	25
25.	Saratoga.........T	12
175.	Sardinia.........P	19
80.	Saturn...........Q	7
160.	Schererville.......E	5
25	Schnellville.........I	23
200.	Scipio...........O	19
50	Scircleville.. L	12
100.	Scotland. ....H	20
25.	Scott...........P	3
821.	Scottsburgh.......O	21
75.	Scottsville.........N	23
25.	Scottville.... ....K	21
40.	Seafield.........H	9
40.	Sedalia.............J	11
50.	Sedan..........S	5
25	Seelyville. ·-.....F	16
33.	Selby....... ......N	6
100.	Sellersburgh ......O	23
125	Selina..........R	12
225.	Sevastopol........M	7
25.	Seward, 12 m S W Warsaw..........N	6
3628.	Seymo r...........N	20
80.	Shadesville ....O	11
20.	Shakapee. 4 m N W Winamac.....J	7
15.	Shakertown, 3 m N W Busseron....E	20

Pop.	Towns—continued.

Pop.	Towns—continued.

Pop.	Towns—continued.		
25.	Springfield ....R		4
30.	Spring Hill ....Q		17
20.	Spring Hill ....E		17
95.	Springport....·... Q		13
40.	Spring Station... G		25
	Springtown, see		
	Marengo . .... K		23
25.	Springtown ... ... S		19
30	Springville .. ..S I		3
15.	Springville, 6 m S E		
	Vernon ......P		19
125.	Springville........ J		20
20.	Spurgeon ....F		24
128	St. Anthony I		23
25.	St. Bernice.......D		15
40	St. Henry ....H		24
30.	St. James ....D		24
25.	St. Joe...........T		6
125	St. John ....E		5
30.	St. Johns...........S		5
25.	St. Johns ....O		17
20.	St. John's ....E		25
23	St. Joseph ....D		25
30.	St. Joseph ....O		23
	St. Joseph's Hill,		
	see St. Joseph... O		23
	St. Joseph Station,		
	see St. Joe .....T		6
75	St. Leon ....T		18
25.	St. Louis, 1 m S		
	Cannelton I		26
30	St. Louis .... O		18
20.	St. Louis Crossing N		18
25.	St. Magdalene.....Q		20
15.	St. Marks I		23
15.	St. Marys ....R		5
45	St. Marys ...... E		16
	St. Marys Station,		
	see St. Marys... E		16
200.	St. Maurice ..... R		17
75.	St. Meinrad........I		24
25.	St. Nicholas, 2 m		
	S W Spades Depot S		18
94	St. Omer ....P		17
425	St. Paul ....P		17
100.	St. Peters ....S		17
25.	St. Philip C		25
30.	St. Wendell's C		25
20.	Stacers............D		24
	Stacer Station,see		
	Stacers .. ..D		24
25.	Stamphers Creek .K		22
45.	Stanford I		19
75	Star............Q		15
228.	Star City.........J		8
25	Stark 3 m N E		
	Knox ....J		6
833.	State Line..........D		12
30.	State Line.........D		9
125.	State Line Station.T		3
25.	State Line Station.D		4
30.	Staughnton, 10 m		
	S E New Castle..Q		14
646.	Staunton..........F		16

Pop.	Towns—continued.		
15.	Steamburgh...... H		4
25.	Steam Corner.... F		13
20.	Steavens Mills. 8 m		
	N Rensselaer. . G		8
30.	Steele, 8 m E Rush-		
	ville .... Q		16
45.	Stendal .... G		24
25.	Steph.nsport .....F		24
37	Steubenville . .... S		4
20.	Steubenville, 3 m S		
	W Ridgeville.... S		12
75.	Stewartsville C		21
200.	Stilesville ....J		16
25	Stillwell..........J		4
	Stillwell Station,		
	see Stillwell.... J		4
178	Stinesville..........J		18
30.	Stips Hill ....R		17
40.	Stockdale ....N		8
25	Stockton ....G		18
150.	Stockwell I		12
25.	Stone ....S		12
75.	Stone Bluff .. ....F		12
30.	Stoners......... S		6
15.	Stone's Crossing, 8		
	m N W White-		
	land. ....M		16
20.	Stony Point.......Q		20
28	Straders..........F		12
	Straughn's Station,		
	see Strawn's .....R		15
40.	Strawn's..........R		15
25.	Strawtown . ....N		13
18.	Stringtown, 3 m E		
	Greenfield ....O		15
30	Sturgeon..........L		7
85.	Sugar Branch .....S		20
25.	Sugar Creek.......N		15
33.	Sugar Grove ......G		12
1913	Sullivan... ......E		19
300.	Sulphur Springs.. Q		13
25	Sulphur Hill, 6 m		
	N E Flat Rock...N		17
20	Sulphur Well.....K		24
	Suman, see Su-		
	manville ....G		4
35.	Sumanville.........G		4
	*Summersville, Gib-		
	son Co.		
25	Summerville, 5 m		
	N Ft. Wayne ... S		7
100.	Summit............S		4
15.	Summit,3 m W Ply-		
	mouth L		6
	Summit, see Mt.		
	Summit..... .....Q		13
30.	Summit............J		15
28	Summit ....O		22
20.	Summit Grove.... E		15
175.	Summitville.... ...P		12
	Sumption, see		
	Sumption Prai-		
	rie...............K		4
25	Sumption Prairie..K		4

Pop.	Towns—continued.		
25.	Sumner	P	16
30.	Sumner	E	12
300.	Sunman	S	18
30	Sunny Side	L	15
15.	Sunny Side	L	15
20.	Swan	R	6
25	Swanville	P	21
175	Sweetsers	O	10
	Sweetsers Station, see Sweetsers	O	10
40.	Swits City	G	19
25.	Sycamore Corner	N	10
38.	Sylvania	F	14
575	Syracuse	O	5
	Tabertown, suburb of Logansport	K	9
25	Taggart's	K	17
15.	Taggarts Sett, 4 m N E Nashville	L	18
30.	Talbot	E	10
45.	Tampico	N	21
25.	Tampico	M	11
15	Tanglewood	R	19
	*Tank, Hendricks Co.		
28.	Tannersville	O	19
30	Tarkeo	Q	18
25	Tarry Hall	M	11
20.	Tar Spring, 7 m W Magnolia	K	24
82.	Tassinong	G	5
	Tassinong Grove, see Tassinong	G	5
25.	Taswell	J	23
15	Taylor, 4 m N E Farmersville	B	25
30	Taylor	E	12
35	Taylor	P	7
25	Taylor's	H	11
	Taylor's Junction, see Taylor's	H	11
	Taylors Station, see Taylor	P	7
175.	Taylorsville	N	18
30	Taylorsville	G	24
20.	Tecumseh	E	16
200.	Teegarden	K	5
2943	Tell City	I	26
100.	Templeton	F	10
	Ten Mile Switch, see Memphis	O	22
40.	Terre Coupee	K	3
25.	Terre Coupee Station	K	3
16101.	Terre Haute	E	17
84.	Tetersburgh	M	12
20.	Texas, 4 m N E Saltillo	L	21
25	Thornlysville, 8 m S E Lebanon	K	13
1368.	Thorntown	J	13
28	Tile Siding	G	13
33.	Tinkerville	E	6

Pop.	Towns—continued.		
25	Tiosa	L	7
125	Tippecanoetown	M	6
1347.	Tipton	M	12
	Tiptonsport, 8 m N E Delphi	J	10
25	Titusville	R	20
30	Tobacco Landing, 14 m S E Corydon	M	24
27.	Tobin's Landing, 8 m S E Cannelton	I	26
20	Tobinsport	J	26
155	Tolleston	E	4
75.	Toronto	E	15
25.	Toto	I	6
200.	Traders Point	L	14
247.	Trafalgar	M	17
90.	Transitville	I	11
25.	Trask	P	11
	Travis, see Travisville	R	9
20.	Travisville	R	9
20.	Treaty	O	9
40.	Trenton	R	11
90	Trenton	S	13
38	Trinity Springs	I	24
25	Troutman's	H	13
704.	Troy	I	25
80.	Troy Siding	E	13
	Troy Station, see Troy Siding	E	13
90	Tunnelton	K	21
37	Turkey Creek	S	4
25.	Turman's Creek	D	18
15.	Turner, 5 m S W Knightsville	G	16
80	Twelve Mile	L	8
20	Twin Corners, 5 m N E Logansport	K	9
330	Tyner City	K	5
25.	Tyners, 8 m W Connersville	S	16
15.	Union, 6 m S E South Bend	L	4
55.	Union	E	22
25.	Union	T	17
2127	Union City	U	12
	Union Corners, see Eaton	Q	11
25.	Union Depot, 4 m N E Vincennes	D	21
80	Union Grove	P	10
825.	Union Mills	I	5
	Union Mills, see Mongo, 7 m S E Lima	Q	8
95.	Unionport	S	13
30.	Uniontown, 5 m N W Bluffton	R	9
20	Uniontown	O	20
27.	Uniontown	K	6
80	Union Village	L	16
15.	Unionville	K	22
20.	Unionville	K	18

Pop.	Towns—continued.		
25.	Unionville, 3 m N E Haskells	H	5
180	Upland	P	11
25.	Upton	B	25
30.	Urbana	O	8
20.	Urbana	T	6
40.	Urmeyville	N	16
25.	Utah, 3 m N W La Grange	Q	4
200.	Utica	P	23
20.	Utica, 4 m N E Wabash	O	9
45.	Valeene	K	23
100.	Valentine	Q	4
15.	Valley	L	21
25.	Valley City	L	25
	Valley City, see New Ross	I	14
30.	Valley Creck, 6 m S W Lebanon	K	13
18.	Valley Mills	L	15
185.	Vallonia	M	20
6614.	Valparaiso	G	5
25.	Van Buren	P	10
125	Van Buren	P	8
275.	Vandalia	H	18
25.	Vanderbilt	F	4
40.	Vanseckle's	K	17
	Van Weddens, see Weisburgh	S	18
340.	Veedersburgh	F	13
	Velonia, see Vallonia	M	20
374.	Vera Cruz	S	9
25.	Vermont, 4 m E Kokomo	M	10
930.	Vernon	P	19
30	Verona, 6 m S W Evansville	D	25
674	Versailles	R	19
25.	Vertland	M	14
20.	Very's Mill, 5 m N W Jefferson-ville	O	24
2189.	Vevay	S	21
25.	Vicksburgh	E	13
308.	Vienna	O	22
25.	Vienna, 9 m E Rushville	Q	16
30	Vienna	T	5
9315	Vincennes	D	21
40.	Vine's Springs	K	19
125.	Vistula	O	3
30.	Volga	P	21
25.	Votaw	T	14
3435.	Wabash	O	9
75.	Wadesville	C	25
27.	Wagne Station	F	20
30.	Wagner's Mills, 10 m S Dover Hill	I	21
25.	Wagoner's Station	M	8
	Wagoner's, see Wagoner's Station	M	8

Pop.	Towns—continued.		
294	Wakarusa	M	4
300	Waldron	O	17
25.	Walesborough	N	19
525	Walkerton	J	5
75	Wallace	G	13
23.	Wallbaum	L	9
135.	Wallen	R	7
120.	Walnut	L	6
25.	Walnut Grove	E	14
34.	Walnut Grove	E	13
25	Walnut Hill	H	13
	Walnut Station, see Walnut	L	6
600.	Walton	L	10
30	Waltz	N	9
625	Wanatah	H	5
25.	Warren, 7 m N W Corydon	M	24
300.	Warren	Q	9
40.	Warren	T	12
	Warren, see Warren Centre	K	8
30.	Warren Centre	K	8
	Warren Station, see Warren	T	12
25.	Warrenton	D	24
15.	Warrickton, 5 m W Boonville	F	25
200	Warrington	P	14
2685.	Warsaw	N	6
451.	Washington	S	14
4856.	Washington	F	21
25.	Waterbury, 3 m N W Rome	J	26
125.	Waterford	O	4
20	Waterford, 2 m N W La Porte	I	4
	Waterford Mills, see Waterford	O	4
30.	Waterloo	S	15
1689	Waterloo	S	5
85.	Waterman	E	14
25	Watson	H	19
30.	Watson	O	23
813.	Waveland	G	14
45.	Waverly	L	16
25.	Waverly	L	9
375	Wawaka	Q	5
25	Wawasa	R	16
40	Wawpecong	M	10
15.	Way, 2 m N E Morris	R	18
20.	Waymansville	M	19
25.	Waynesburgh	O	18
20.	Wayneaville	N	19
577.	Waynetown	G	13
25.	Wayport	J	18
50.	Wea	H	11
30.	Weaton, 8 m N La-fayette	H	11
28	Webber's	I	8
40.	Webster	T	14
65.	Webster	O	5
25.	Weddlesville	L	20

Pop.	Towns—continued.		
225.	Weisburgh	S	18
	Wellington, see		
	Willington	M	14
30.	Wellsboro	I	5
20.	Wellsburg	R	9
15.	Wesley	G	13
	West Baden, see		
	West Baden		
	Springs	J	22
25	West BadenSprings	J	22
20.	West Buena Vista	E	22
40.	West Chester	T	10
25.	West Creek	E	6
20.	West Delphi, 1 m		
	W Delphi	J	10
420	Westfield	M	13
30	West Fork	J	24
28	West Franklin	C	26
24.	West Grove	S	14
20.	West Hampton, 2		
	m N E La Porte	I	4
84.	West Junction	S	7
25	West Kinderhook	N	12
35.	Westland	O	15
20.	Westland	I	16
2255.	West Lebanon	E	12
90.	West Liberty	N	11
40.	West Liberty	S	10
25.	West Logan, 1 m N		
	Logansport	K	9
30.	West Logansport,		
	1 m W Logans-		
	port	K	9
	West Middleton,		
	see Middleton	L	11
25	West Mills	Q	13
15.	West Milton, 4 m		
	S W Danville	J	15
40.	West Newton	L	16
20.	West Newton Sta-		
	tion	L	15
25.	West Ossian	R	8
125	West Point	G	11
30.	West Point Station	G	11
302	Westport	P	18
20	West Salem, 4 m		
	N W Martinsville	R	17
25	West Shoals	I	12
15.	West Union, 2 m		
	N E Montezuma	E	15
18.	West Union, 11 m		
	N W Edwards-		
	port	F	21
846	Westville	H	4
95.	Wheatland	F	21
25.	Wheaton	H	11
30.	Wheatonville	E	24
25.	Wheatville,3 m N E		
	Denver	M	8
65.	Wheeler	F	4
47.	Wheeling	P	11
25	Wheeling	K	10
180.	Whitcomb	T	17
20.	White Creek	N	19

Pop.	Towns—continued.		
150.	White Hall	I	18
175.	Whiteland	M	16
25.	White Lick, 10 m		
	S E Lebanon	K	13
30.	Whiteport, 2 m N		
	Francesville	H	8
475.	Whitestown	K	13
20.	White River, 8 m		
	N E Richmond	T	14
48	Whitesville	I	14
155	Whitewater	U	14
25	Whitings	E	3
30.	Wickliffe	J	23
20.	Wigg's	N	18
28.	Wilbur	J	16
35	Wild Cat	J	11
25.	Wild Cat	H	11
30	Williams	S	8
	Williams, see Wil-		
	liams Station	F	16
190	Williamsburgh	T	14
100.	Williamsburgh	M	17
25	William's Crossing	L	17
30.	Williamsport, 10 m		
	S W Rushville	Q	16
900	Williamsport	F	12
230.	Williamsport	S	8
25.	Williams Station	F	16
30	Williamstown	Q	17
30.	Willington	M	14
20.	Wilmington	T	19
15.	Willmington	T	5
25	Wilmot	P	6
30.	Willow Branch	P	14
28	Willow Valley	I	21
18.	Wilson's	N	23
30.	Wilsons	N	10
25.	Wilsons Creek, 8 m		
	S E Purcells	D	22
1046.	Winamac	J	7
2129	Winchester	T	13
741.	Windfall	N	11
25.	Windsor	R	13
30	Winfield	F	5
23.	Winfield	B	24
15	Winona, 12 m N W		
	Portland	T	11
25.	Winslow	H	5
200.	Winslow	F	23
30.	Winterroud	O	17
40.	Wintersville	Q	18
25.	Wirt	Q	21
30.	Wirt Station	Q	21
180	Wolcott	G	9
	Wolcott Station,		
	see Wolcott	G	9
675	Wolcottville	Q	4
75	Wolf Creek	L	6
75.	Wolf Lake	Q	6
30.	Woodbank	M	14
25	Woodburn	T	7
35	Woodbury	N	14
88.	Woodland	L	4
25	Woods	T	13

Pop.	Towns—continued.		
30.	Woodville...... ... P	14
20.	Woodville.........K	21
28	Woodville......... J	10
35.	Woodville, 9 m S E Brownstown.....M	20
18.	Wood Yard.......J	18
20	Woody's Corner ..F	14
25.	Wooster............O	6
45.	Woostertown......O	21
30.	Worcester.........O	4
15.	Worth, 3 m S Celestine...............I	23
18.	Worth............L	24
-1272.	Worthington...... H	19
	Worthington, see Worthington Crossing... ....R	10
40.	Worthington Crossing. ....R	10
25.	Worthsville......M	16
31.	Wrays, 5 m N E Shelbyville...... O	16
23.	Wright............F	19
30.	Wrights ....G	25
25.	Wright's Corner .T	19
15	Wrights Corner . R	4
20.	Wrightsdale, 5 m N W Shelbyville.O	17
30	Wyandotte..... . I	11
185	Wymansville, 9 m W Jonesville... N	19
25.	Wynn ... . T	17
18.	Wyoming, 4 m N E Bradford.........H	8

Pop.	Towns—continued		
30	Wynnsborough.. L	24
25	Xenia, 4 m S E Delphi... .. ..J	10
945.	Xenia............N	10
80.	Yankeetown.. . F	26
25.	Yellow Bank. ... S	17
20.	York, 5 m S Princeton...... ... .D	23
90	York Centre, 10 m N E Angola.... T	4
569.	Yorktown.........P	13
35.	Yorktown, 4 m E Corwin.......... H	12
25.	Yorkville........T	18
150	Young America, 12 m S Logansport............ K	9
30.	Young's Creek... K	22
25.	Youngstown, 3 m W Crawfordsville...... .....H	13
45	Youngstown.... . E	17
90.	Yountsville.......H	13
285	Zanesville, 14 m S W Ft. Wayne. S	7
40.	Zanesville.........R	8
125	Zenas..,........,.. Q	19
	Zenor's Landing, see Rosewood....N	25
30.	Zigler.... .....K	3
25.	Zinsburgh ....O	13
957.	Zionsville.........L	14

INDIANA—APPENDIX.

RAILROADS.

Indianapolis, Delphi & Chicago.

Rensselaer (G 8) to Bradford (H 8).

Havana, Rantoul & Eastern.

West Lebanon (E 12) to Fisher, Ill. (S 14).

TOWNS.

Hanging Grove, 8 m S E Rensselaer (G 8).
Lee, 3 m N W Bradford (H 8).
Pleasant Ridge, 4 m S E Rensselaer (G 8).

—THE—
BANKERS' DIRECTORY

OF THE

United States and Canada.

A most useful publication for business houses. The work is an octavo volume of 400 pages, handsomely printed and bound,

CONTAINING:

A list of Banks, Bankers and Savings Banks in the United States, with names of Officers, Capital, and Correspondents.

A list of Banks and Bankers in Canada, with names of Officers and United States Correspondents.

A list of Cashiers of National, State and Private Banks.

A list of Assistant Cashiers of National, State and Private Banks.

The Clearing Houses in the United States, with names of Officers.

A list of Brokers in New York City.

The Commercial Laws of each State and Territory, including the Laws relating to Insolvency, Interest, Taxes, Notes and Bills of Exchange, etc.

A list of reliable Commercial Lawyers.

(The publishers have inserted only the names of those Attorneys recommended by Banks and Bankers in their own locality, thus making the list to contain only such names as have the confidence of the community in which they reside.)

Parties making their own collections and whose business covers a wide extent of territory, will appreciate the special features of this new compilation, and find it an invaluable reference book for office use.

PRICE, THREE DOLLARS

Sent Prepaid, by Mail, to any Address.

RAND, McNALLY & CO., Publishers,

CHICAGO, ILL.